# THE CHICAGO BANK ROBBERIES

## Book 1 of The Motorbike Gang Series

## Matthew & Zachary Pierre

PIERRE BOOKS

Cover Design: Sampath Fernando

Interior Design: Matthew Pierre

ISBN: 979-8-9927965-0-6

Pierre Books LLC

1903 West 8th St PMB# 274

Erie, PA 16505

*Dedicated to the Lord.*

*Just as we are Your*

*workmanship, thank you for*

*allowing us to create this*

*piece of art.*

# Table of Contents

# Character Profile

### Jack Wesley

Age: 10 | Schooled Publicly

Strength: Boldness and Persistence

Jack is the founder and club leader of the Motorbike Gang. He loves to get to the bottom of things, but can be a little rash when doing so.

### Carly Hankerson

Age: 10 | Schooled Publicly

Strength: Excellent Photography Skills

Carly is Jack's best friend and co-founder of the club. She's very questioning, loves photography and uses her camera skills to photograph important clues during investigation.

### William (Billy) Jones

Age: 11 | Homeschooled

Strength: Logic and Technological Skills

Billy is one of the smartest people in Westport, Michigan, and a valuable asset to the club. He loves to tinker with old machines and invent clever contraptions. Some

work and help his friends, while others don't turn out very well.

## Rachel Karlson

Age: 12 | Homeschooled

Strength: Mental Strength and Caution

Rachel is basically the mother of the club, being the oldest of the only two female members. She keeps the boys in line, and takes the most caution during investigation. Rachel spends her free time practicing archery and baking.

## Mike Michaels

Age: 12 | Cyber-Schooled

Strength: Open-Mindedness and Tech-Savvy

Mike is the club's self-proclaimed conspiracy theorist. He spends a lot of time on the Internet and comes up with plenty of wacky and (mostly) useless conspiracies, but is very useful in emergency situations. Mike is a cyberschooler, plays basketball, and aspires to join the military when he's older.

## Jerry Smith

Age: 13 | Homeschooled

Strength: Vigilance

Alert Jerry is the club's lookout. He's a clever sleuth and loves to spend his free time painting.

## Robby Green

Age: 13 | Homeschooled

Strength: Interrogation

Robby is a pessimist, but his tendency to look at the worst aspects of things has given him a valuable detective skill. Robby is the eldest member of the Motorbike Gang, and has a twin sister who leads a rival club, the E-Bike Gang.

## Samuel (Sam) Jones

Age: 17 | Homeschooled

Strength: Undercover Operation

Billy's older brother Sam isn't technically a member of the club, only being around to watch the kids. But since he's pretty much an adult and has a driver's license, he and his motorcycle are arguably the club's best resources.

# Chapter 1

The sun hung low in the pink sky, shooting its rays across the small town of Westport, Michigan. The rooster was hit first and screamed out of routine. Its shrill pitch was heard by ten-year-old Jack Wesley, who groaned, rolled over, and went back to sleep.

An hour later, Jack mumbled, grumbled, and sat up. He sat there for a minute, letting his body adjust to the morning. Jack changed his clothes and went downstairs, where his parents were having a cup of coffee and reading the local newspaper.

"Hey Jack," his dad said without the usual smile. "You slept in today and missed the bus."

"What time is it?" Jack asked, unsure if his dad was joking or not.

"7:15."

"Oh no! Why didn't you wake me up? My alarm is broken."

"I called you earlier, but you didn't answer," Mom answered. "We assumed you had woken up and were getting ready, until the bus just rolled past the house."

"I better bring breakfast to go if I want to make it to school!"

Jack was always prepared. He made breakfast to-go every night before bed. He warmed up his breakfast, put it in a paper bag, and grabbed his backpack. "Bye, Mom and Dad! I'll be home after school!"

Jack grabbed his motorbike from the garage. As he started to ride, he noticed Carly Hankerson coming out of her backyard with her bike.

"Hi, Carly. Why aren't you on the bus?"

Carly Hankerson was Jack's best friend. She had hazel eyes and shoulder-length brown hair. Jack and Carly had been friends since they could remember, since their fathers were also close friends. Carly's grandparents were originally from Mexico. Carly was the same age as Jack and lived only a few houses away from the Wesleys. She loved photography, taking her camera everywhere she went.

Carly frowned at Jack's question. "When I came outside, the bus had just driven past my house. What about you?"

"I slept in way too late, and missed it, too. I was up longer than usual last night writing my report."

"Well, we better get going!"

Jack and Carly arrived at school at 7:29.

"Nice going, Jack. One minute early," said one of Jack's friends.

At school, Jack had a final report due on the importance of history. It was the second-to-last day of school, making it an important assignment for him to complete.

After several kids gave their reports, it was his turn. As Jack walked to the front of the room, he could feel his classmates staring at his neck. He stopped at the teacher's desk and turned around. He gulped, and looked at Carly, who gave him a thumbs-up and smiled.

"I think the importance of history is simple," Jack started his report. "History is the remembrance of the past. For example, police have records of every case, arrest, and warrant. They don't throw it in the trash. They keep it for evidence. Medical centers don't throw away patients' records, they keep them in case they ever have to bring them up again.

"History is important because you never know when you have to pull it up again. If you want to be an explorer, study the way of exploring, the history of past explorations. If you want to be a doctor, studying basic procedures proven in the past to work is a good start."

Jack's classmates applauded as he sat down. He was glad his report was over. Jack took his seat and glanced over at Carly, who smiled as she got up to give her own report.

After Carly and a few others gave their reports, the bell rang for lunch. The students crammed their books into their desks and headed for the cafeteria.

Toward the end of lunch, the school bully, Todd Bailey, swaggered to where Jack and Carly were eating. He was 14 years old, had curly hair, and always wore heavy hiking boots, even though he never hiked. Jack always thought it was to intimidate kids.

"One of your friends told me about your report," Todd sneered. "I'm gonna make a history of all the punches I owe you. And I'll start by adding two punches for the way you're looking at me."

*Have you ever punched a kid?* Jack wondered.

Another kid yelled, "How about deducting two punches for failing science class last year?"

Todd whirled around. "Who said that?"

The bell rang right at that moment, and all the kids went to the next class. On the way to math class, Carly slapped Jack on the back. "Wow, wasn't that kid brave to speak up to Todd like that?"

"Yeah, and the bell rang just in time, too."

When the afternoon classes ended, Jack and Carly rode their bikes home. They talked about upcoming events, Todd and the way he swaggered, and their grades on the math test.

"I'm telling you, Jack, I got 100 on mine." Carly swerved close to Jack's front tire.

"No way!" Jack jerked his tire away from Carly. "I always get an 83 or something like that."

"Then study more at home. We're almost there anyway."

On the way home, Jack and Carly rode past a man starting to cross the street. The man wasn't paying attention and nearly collided with Jack. Jack swerved in time, but his bike slammed into the stranger's briefcase.

"Hey!" Jack steadied his bike by putting his feet down. "Watch where you're going, mister!"

"Why don't you try watching where you're going!"

All the papers in the stranger's briefcase had flown out and scattered across the street.

"We're sorry." Carly hopped off her bike and started to reach for the papers. "Can we help you pick up your papers?"

"Why don't you mind your own business!" The man frantically began stuffing papers into his briefcase.

He moved sideways trying to conceal what was written on them. Jack spied a few papers with the words *stolen* and *hide*, and a mysterious note. He grabbed a few sheets that had blown away from the man. The man grabbed the notes from Jack's hand and rushed off with stray papers sticking out of the briefcase.

Jack and Carly couldn't believe their eyes. The encounter with the mysterious stranger piqued their interest.

"Did you see those notes in his briefcase? Let's follow him!" Jack said excitedly.

"Shouldn't we be heading home?" Carly asked.

"We've got plenty of time before dinner." Jack revved up his bike and started to go after the stranger. Carly followed reluctantly.

A few blocks away, Jack and Carly saw the man get on a bus.

"Now how are we going to follow him?" Carly asked.

"Let's get on the bus," Jack suggested.

"Are you crazy?"

But Jack had already chained his bike to a pole. "The bus driver comes back around here anyway. We'll just see where the man goes and come back around here."

Before Carly could protest, Jack started running toward the bus. Carly sighed and followed him.

Jack paid for their fare, and they moved to the back of the bus. They took seats two rows behind the man with the briefcase.

"I have a bad feeling about this," Carly whispered.

"Then why did you come?" Jack retorted.

"You couldn't go alone."

Half an hour later, the bus stopped at the Westport Airport just outside of town. The man with the briefcase got up and hurried to leave the bus. A slip of paper fell out of his briefcase and landed on the floor of the bus.

Jack picked up the sheet before it got trampled by new passengers. It was a receipt of purchase for a plane ticket to Chicago.

"Carly, we're going to Chicago on vacation tomorrow!" Jack whispered, showing Carly the paper. Jack and Carly's families, along with their friends, were visiting Chicago for their fathers' class reunion.

Carly's eyes grew wide with excitement. "That's right!"

"I wonder why the man wouldn't let us help him pick up his papers, though."

"Maybe he's hiding something, and he doesn't want the public to know."

# Chapter 2

"Who was that man?" Carly's eyes were still bugging out as they rode their bikes home.

"I don't know, but we need to find out. I saw a paper in his briefcase that said, 'Meet at Lily's Cafe, 6/11, at 5' and one paper said, 'stolen' and another said, 'hide.' This guy is up to no good, I know it."

"Maybe the numbers on the paper are a date," Carly pointed out to Jack. "The numbers 6 and 11 could be June 11th, and the number 5 could be 5 o'clock."

"Maybe," Jack shrugged.

The two discussed what they should do during the ride.

"I wonder if I'll see him when we go on our vacation," Jack said, pulling his bike into the garage.

"I'll also keep my eyes open just in case." Carly waved. "Goodnight."

As Jack walked up the steps of his home, a figure was lurking in the shadows of his driveway, watching him. Whoever it was bumped into one of the trash cans, startling Jack. He jumped and turned to scan the driveway. No one was there.

Jack's heart raced as he pulled out his key from his pocket. But Jack's nerves caused him to drop it accidentally. He squatted to pick it up, watching the driveway. Jack grabbed the key, struggling to put it in the keyhole of the door with his shaky hands, then twisted the doorknob.

"Mom, Dad, I'm home!" Jack shouted as he entered the living room.

Mom hurried into the living room. "Where were you? Dinner's almost ready, and you need to set the table."

"Sorry, Mom. I was—" Jack hesitated, not wanting to mention his visit to the airport. "—uh, got distracted with a friend."

Mom gave him a stern look. "Jack, it's nearly 6 o'clock. We'll talk about this later. Now go set the table."

Jack placed his backpack down on the couch. He went to the kitchen sink, washed his hands, then grabbed the dishes to set the table.

During dinner, Dad asked, "So Jack, how was school today?"

"It was okay." Jack picked at his food, too excited to eat. "But I can't wait for the last day of school tomorrow."

As they ate, Jack asked, "Dad, can I spend the night at Jerry's house? Tomorrow, I don't really have classes because it's the last day of school. And Jerry's already finished with homeschool this year. Not to mention, some of the gang are going to be at his house."

"What gang?" asked Dad. "You know what we said about joining gangs."

Jack groaned. "It's been over a year since we put the gang together, and you still don't remember the name?"

"He's joking," said Mom.

"So can I *please* go to Jerry's house?" Jack begged.

Dad looked at Mom.

"Sure," said Mom, "but you need to be back at the house by 7 o'clock tomorrow morning if

you're going to be able to eat breakfast and still catch the bus. And you also need to behave at Jerry's house."

"Thanks!" Jack ran from the dinner table to pack his clothes. He called Carly with his walkie-talkie and told him that his parents were letting him go over to Jerry's.

"That's great!" Carly said. "We're going to have a blast!"

"I'll see you there," said Jack. "Jack out."

A few minutes later, Jack rode his motorbike over to Jerry's house. When he got there, Jerry had already prepared the living room for the sleepover. He had popped the popcorn, set blankets on the floor, got the TV ready, and brought some fizzing drinks.

Soon, Samuel and Billy Jones joined the sleepover. Billy was a member of the Motorbike Gang, along with Jack, Carly, and a few others.

Sam, Billy's 17-year-old brother, was really only involved with the club to supervise the gang. Sam and Billy were both homeschooled, as well as most of the club.

The kids settled in, and soon began their mini meeting. Jack told the gang about his and Carly's encounter with the stranger with the briefcase.

"We learned that he was taking a plane to Chicago!" Jack blurted out in excitement.

"Did you put a tracking device on him?" 11-year-old Billy pushed up his round glasses that were always slipping down his nose. He was very smart and loved to tinker with old machines and invent clever contraptions.

"How would we put a tracking device on him?" Jack placed his hands on his hips.

"And where would they get one?" 13-year-old Jerry added.

Billy frowned. "I told you to take one of my latest models with you just in case. You told me they were useless."

"We've never had to track anyone before," Jack shot back.

"You said my inventions are impractical."

"Because they are!"

"Guys, calm down," Sam said. "First, you shouldn't be spying on random strangers. Second, since I know you're not going to listen, Chicago is a big city. It isn't likely that you're going to find him."

"We can still try," Jack said.

"I agree," said Jerry. "If he is a thief, he needs to be arrested."

Sam rolled his eyes. "Whatever."

Jerry grabbed the remote and flipped to the news channel. The evening news had just started.

"On tonight's news we have reports of valuable jewels stolen in California," the

newswoman on screen began. "A renowned archeological team found rare gemstones during a dig in southern Asia. The team partnered with a large mining corporation to excavate and import the jewels worth millions of dollars. But during the transport to a museum in California, the jewels were stolen. The theft of such a closely guarded project has baffled the authorities."

After a few more minutes of watching, Jerry turned off the TV.

"I read about those jewels online before," Billy said. "It's a real disappointment that they're stolen. We may never get to see them again."

"Do you think the man with the briefcase is involved with the theft?" asked Jack.

"Now Jack, don't start jumping to conclusions." Billy pushed up his glasses again.

As the kids talked some more, ate popcorn, and played games, the clock ticked, and minutes turned into hours. Soon, they all were tired and fell into a deep sleep.

# Chapter 3

The next morning, the boys packed up their bags, and left Jerry's house. "My mom says sorry she leaves for work early, or she would have made breakfast for us," Jerry said. "I mean, Dad's cooking is *edible,* but. . ." He shook his head slowly.

"No problem," the other boys shrugged.

A car beeped outside.

"There's our mom," Sam said, looking out the window. "Bye guys."

Jack rode his motorbike home. When he got home, his house was filled with the smell of sizzling bacon.

In the kitchen, Mom was cooking up a delicious breakfast of bacon, scrambled eggs, and a stack of hot pancakes. Jack took a shower, changed into his school clothes, and ran down the steps to his seat at the table. A nice plate of food was waiting for him.

"So, Jack," Mom said as she removed three pancakes from the pan, "how was your sleepover?"

"It was great," Jack mumbled between mouthfuls. He gobbled down bacon, eggs, and pancakes drenched in syrup.

Jack dashed out the door, his backpack dangling from one of his shoulders. The bus stopped on the other side of the street.

Jack ran across the street, where Carly was getting on with a few other neighborhood kids. Jack sat with Carly on the left side of the third row. No one else ever sat in it, knowing that it was their favorite spot.

As the bus rolled down the street, it bumped and jumped, making it a fun, but painful ride. The bus stopped a couple of blocks down the street to pick up a few other kids.

Jack and Carly waved to the group. They were fellow classmates.

During the ride, Jack and Carly felt liquid jiggling on their heads. Dripping down their faces, Jack felt the weird substance. Jack looked at Carly and saw yellow egg yolk sliding down her forehead. *Oh no!* He saw the same thing on his own shirt and peeked behind him.

The school bully Todd Bailey was laughing with one of his buddies, Skip, who was hollering at the sight of the kids.

"Look!" Todd pointed, shaking with laughter, "they're egg men!"

Jack was furious, and so was Carly. Giggles were contagious, and soon everybody was laughing at the "egg men." As the kids got off the bus, one child told the bus driver about the prank, and Todd got a stern scolding. He was five minutes late for class from having to clean the seats on the bus that had egg yolk residue on them.

After a fun last day of school, the students ran out the door, swinging their backpacks and joking with their friends.

Jack found Todd leaving the vending machine with a soda in his hand, and hurried to confront him.

Jack pushed his finger in Todd's chest. "That prank on the bus wasn't funny!"

"First, don't touch me." Todd swatted Jack's finger. "Second, I was playing around. Besides, it's the last day of school, so you can't do anything."

Todd tried to step around Jack, but Jack stayed in front.

"Get out of my way!" Todd snarled.

"No." Jack dug in his heels. "I'm not moving 'til you apologize."

The bully dropped the soda can and shoved him off the sidewalk, then swaggered off.

Frustrated, Jack picked up and threw the soda can across the street, hitting Todd. Before the teenager could react, Jack ran as fast as he could back into the crowd of kids.

When he got home, Dad was in the kitchen, listening to the radio and adding up the bills. Mom was at work during the day, and Dad's work shift was late during the night. Jack went to his room, changed his clothes, and ran to the back door.

"Dad, I'm going to Mike's treehouse!"

"Just be back by 5 o'clock tonight." Dad looked up for a second from his pile of bills. "We need to prepare to leave for the airport."

Jack rushed to the side of the house and grabbed his motorbike. He sped off, forgetting to put his helmet on. It took him five minutes to get there. He parked his motorbike in the driveway of the Michaels, hurried through the backyard, and climbed up the treehouse ladder.

Inside the treehouse, Billy sat with two more members of the gang. Mike Michaels and Rachel Karlson were both 12 years old. Instead of attending public school like Jack and Carly, Rachel was homeschooled, and Mike was enrolled in cyberschool.

"Where's the rest of the gang?" Jack asked.

"They haven't arrived yet." Billy pushed up his glasses. He checked his watch and added, "But they've got 4 minutes and 37 seconds before they're considered tardy."

Shortly after the comment, Sam pulled his cycle into Mike's driveway, and climbed up into the treehouse. Soon, Carly and Jerry came. The only one left was Robby Green.

"I wonder where Robby is," said Carly.

After a short argument, they decided to wait five more minutes for Robby.

After five minutes, a girl walked into the backyard, carrying two flags. One was white, and the other was blue and orange, with a green line separating the two colors.

"Oh no," Jerry, the club's lookout, moaned, "it's a member of the E-Bike Gang."

He looked at the messenger's flags. "But it looks like they're coming in peace."

The E-Bike Gang was a rival club. Earlier in the history of the Motorbike Gang, a big feud had sprung up between the members, causing Emma Green (Robby's twin sister), Kevin and Ellie Thompson, and Timmy Smith (Jerry's cousin) to

form their own gang. The two gangs were competitive foes in the clubs.

Mike leaped out of the treehouse, twisting in a somersault, and landed in front of the rival member. "What do you want?"

"I come in peace," the messenger thrust the white flag in Mike's face.

Mike stepped back and looked up. "Will we grant her permission to enter?"

"What do you think, Jack?" Carly turned her head.

Jack thought for a moment, then shouted down to Mike, "Yes!"

"Permission to enter the treehouse granted." Mike pointed to the ladder. The girl carefully put down her flags.

She climbed up the creaking ladder, then stepped inside. Mike stayed close to her, watching to make sure there was no surprise attack.

"What is your message, Ellie?" Jack asked.

"My leader, Emma, sent me," Ellie replied.

"Why?" Jack stepped close to her.

"To tell you that Robby is sick. He has a small fever and needs to be in bed for a couple of days."

For a moment nobody said anything.

Carly spoke up. "Well, thanks for telling us. You can leave now."

The girl started for the ladder, but then she whirled back around.

"One more thing." Ellie put her face in Jack's.

Everyone's eyes immediately returned to her.

"The E-Bike Gang is out to get you!"

With those final words, she climbed down the ladder. Mike followed her until she left the backyard, then climbed back up to join the others.

"We need to be prepared for any attacks," Jack said. He banged his gavel. "For now, though, let's begin our meeting. Let's say the pledge."

Everyone stood and recited, "I pledge allegiance to the Motorbike Gang, promising to loyally fulfill my duties, stand up for my fellow clubmates, and—"

"Fight against overly-priced ice-pops at the corner store!" Mike interrupted, once again ruining the pledge.

Jack sighed. "Can we deal with this *after* the pledge?"

"Ok, sorry."

The pledge continued. "—and take care of my motorbike, so help me God."

After reciting the pledge, Jack said, "We need to discuss a more detailed plan to find that man Carly and I ran into yesterday."

"What man?" Rachel asked.

Jack and Carly quickly told Rachel and Mike about the stranger they had bumped into.

"Maybe the man's a foreign spy, trying to overthrow the government!" Mike jumped up and waved his hand. "Or he could be a part of an international ring of gangs that steal rare gems,

animal skins, or elephant tusks, and smuggle them across the globe! And then sell them on the black market or disguised on the Internet. I saw an ad one day that said—"

"First, I highly doubt any of those ideas are true," Rachel interrupted. "And second, is investigating a suspicious stranger a good idea?"

"I kinda get your point," Mike agreed. "He seems sketchy."

"We're going on vacation tomorrow morning," Carly said. "We'll use caution if we see him, but there's no telling what we might uncover. And if we do find him involved with some criminal activity—"

"We can't just do nothing," Jack finished.

"Yes, you can," Sam said. "You'll tell the police and leave it to them."

"But what do we do here?" asked Mike.

"Man the treehouse, especially while we're gone," Jack said. "We'll call you when we get there. Be ready to answer a call at, say . . . 3:15 tomorrow afternoon."

"Good idea, Jack," Rachel said, "I'll tell Robby about our plans."

"Great." Jack hit the gavel on the podium. "Meeting adjourned."

Later that evening, the Wesleys and their friends boarded the plane to Chicago. When they arrived, they checked in at Rosedale Hotel and went to sleep.

# Chapter 4

The next day, Jack contacted his friends back home using his smartwatch. "Hi, Mike, Rachel, and Robby. How are you guys doing?"

"I'm doing great," Rachel replied. "How's the pizza in Chicago?"

"We haven't tried it yet. But, deep dish, here I come!"

Mike laughed. "What are you guys doing now?"

"We're on our way to the arcade across the street from the hotel now."

"I thought Carly didn't like airplanes," Robby said between sneezes. "Was she okay?"

"Yeah," Jack chuckled. "She only threw up once. I'm glad we got off in time, or she would have thrown up again."

"Okay, guys," Mike groaned, "I've gotta go. My mom asked me to get some groceries from the store. I hope your vacation goes well, Jack."

"Thanks, Mike. Goodbye, guys."

As Jack turned his watch off, he heard a door open behind him. Jack spun around and leapt out of the way.

"Hey," he yelled to the person, "you almost hit me!"

"Guess I didn't see you," the person sneered, turning to face Jack.

When he saw the boy, the man quickly turned and sped down the hall in the other direction,

swinging a large briefcase with a diamond mark on the front. Jack stared open-mouthed. The man was the same stranger Jack had bumped into in Westport!

The arcade could wait! Jack ran into his room. Carly was sitting on the bed fixing her camera.

"Carly, I saw the mysterious man with the briefcase!" Jack blurted.

"What?" The news shocked Carly.

"It's true. The man opened the door behind me, and nearly slammed it into me. When he recognized who I was, he hurried down the hall. I'm going after him."

"Take my camera." Carly handed him the small silver camera she had been fixing. "Maybe you can get a shot of him without him noticing."

"I wish we had our motorbikes right now."

Carly nodded glumly.

Jack pocketed the camera and ran down the hall. When he turned to the right and got to the front desk, he sprinted for the door. Jack looked in both directions, and he saw the man turn left at the corner.

Jack ran after him. He followed the man, being cautious not to get too close nor too far. Jack watched the man enter a clothing store. He ran to the window, shot a photo of him, then slipped through the door without being noticed. The man was looking at some ties near one of the checkout counters. Jack pretended to look at some sunglasses, and to hide suspicion, grabbed a pair and went to the counter. Praying the man wouldn't notice him, Jack placed his order on the counter.

The cashier took the glasses and scanned them, then placed them in a small bag and said, "That'll be 97 cents."

Jack pulled his wallet out of his pocket and opened it, surprised to see $30 in it. He then remembered that his dad gave it to him to spend. Forgetting the cost, thinking about the man he was tracking, Jack placed 50 cents on the counter.

The cashier said in annoyance, "That's only 50 cents, boy."

Hearing the comment, the man with the briefcase turned to see who it was. Jack quickly dropped his wallet, some change, and a few other items out of his pocket. Bending down to pick them up, Jack hid his face from the man. He slowly picked the items up, and the stranger walked over to another counter to pay for a few ties.

Jack gave the cashier 47 more cents, apologized for the mix-up, and then left the shop. He put the glasses on, and turned toward the street, drinking from the water bottle that had been in his pocket. When the man left the shop,

Jack waited a few seconds for him to walk down the sidewalk, then turned and stalked him.

The stranger turned into an alleyway, walking all the way to the end of it. Jack had to take off his glasses to see him. He placed a folded note sticking out of a trash can and turned to leave. Jack started walking back down the way he came, until the man left the alleyway.

Jack ran into the alley and grabbed the note. He stuffed it into his pocket and hurried to catch up to the man. He yanked the walkie-talkie out of his back pocket and called Carly.

"Yes?" came Carly's voice on the walkie-talkie.

"I'm still trailing the man, and the signs say we're on Maple Street and crossing Homer Street. I found a message the man planted in a back alley. I haven't read it yet, though. It's hot out here, I ran out of water, and my throat is parched. Can you meet me at Peach Street with some water?"

"Okay," Carly replied. "Carly out."

Jack then texted Billy, Jerry, and Sam and asked them to meet up with him also.

A few minutes later, Carly and Jack were on Peach Street. Carly remembered the water. Jack quickly drained a bottle, then tossed it in the trash before grabbing another.

"Man," Carly commented, "you're drinking like a thirsty camel!"

Jack wiped his brow. "It's so hot out here." After he finished his third bottle, he turned to Carly. "We need to keep trailing the man."

"Right," Carly agreed. "Did you take any photos of him?"

"Only a few."

"What about the message?"

"It's right here." Jack unfolded the paper.

The two read it carefully.

"It's just a receipt," Carly moaned in disappointment.

"Let's keep following the man." Jack threw the paper back into the trash can.

The two hurried across the street just in time to see the man turn a corner. They sprinted to catch up with him. When they turned the corner, Carly checked her watch.

"It's 4:56," she said to Jack. "Four minutes until the man's meeting!"

"And we don't have time to get there," Jack looked over his shoulder and saw the man get into a taxi.

"Hey Jack, look over there!"

Jack looked across the street and saw two bicycles leaning against a telephone pole. A sign next to them said "Free."

"Ooh!" Jack squealed in delight. "Just what we need!"

Carly's watch beeped just then. As she paused to check her messages, Jack started running across the street.

"Jack, wait up," Carly called from on the sidewalk.

Just then, Carly heard the roar of a car engine. She looked up. The car was headed straight for Jack!

# Chapter 5

"Jack, look out!" Carly warned.

Jack looked over and saw the speeding car. Knowing he wouldn't have enough time to run, he put up his hands and closed his eyes in fright. The car braked hard and swerved to Jack's right, barely missing him.

"Hey, watch it!" Carly rushed to the car window, steaming with rage. "You almost hit Jack!"

"Why don't you pay attention to the light," the man snarled as he pointed to the traffic light. "It's green!"

Jack and Carly looked over at the light. It was green.

"Sorry, sir," Jack apologized.

The two ran across the rest of the street. They examined the bikes.

"Good condition ten-speed bikes for free!" Carly exclaimed. "What a deal!"

Jack and Carly grinned as they hopped on their new bikes.

"Do you have a map?" Jack asked Carly.

"No, but I have GPS on my watch."

"Oh, right. Me too."

They crossed a street, then made a right on the next block. Up ahead, three boys pedaled on

bicycles like Jack and Carly's. It was Sam, Billy, and Jerry.

"What are you two doing riding out in downtown Chicago by yourselves?" Sam asked sternly. "You could be in big trouble if your parents found out about this. Not to mention the dangers you could have gotten into out here."

"Sorry," Jack said grimly, "But we needed to follow the man with the briefcase."

Carly noticed the other boys' bikes. "Where did you get those nice wheels?"

Sam stopped his bike. "The lady over on Maple Street. I figured it'd be quicker to ride to wherever you all want to go than walk."

"They were priced way under their worth." Billy pushed his glasses up on his nose. "I calculated the prices of a bike like that, including the scratches, and they totaled out to be worth, in this condition, $45.00!"

"Where did you get yours?" Jerry asked Jack and Carly.

"We got ours for free!" Jack said. "They were against a telephone pole with a 'free' sign next to them."

"Guys," said Carly, "don't forget we have to get to Lily's bakery in time to hear the meeting."

"Right," the others agreed.

Billy looked at his wristwatch. "But calculating traveling top speed and maximum wait time for traffic and pedestrians, we will miss the first six minutes of the meeting."

"Well then, let's go." Jack sped off, the gang following.

When they got to the bakery, as Billy predicted, they were six minutes late. After hiding their bikes in an alley near the shop, they pretended to be rude, nonchalant street kids.

Jerry took his shirt off, revealing a white tank top. Jack put on the sunglasses he bought from

the store. Billy bought a plastic chain near the entrance of the store, while Sam tied his hoodie around his waist. The boys ruffled their hair to look rough, and Sam pulled up one of his sleeves to show off his muscles.

When they walked in, they saw a few tables, and a small counter to their left. Carly and Billy walked over to the cashier to place their orders. The others went to find a table.

"I can see the man with the briefcase," Jerry said, looking over. "He's by himself, with a coffee and two donuts."

Jack leaned in close and whispered, "Keep watching."

As Jerry watched the man, Carly and Billy soon came over with a large box. "Ten confectionery desserts," Billy said, "two for each of us."

"Why do you always use big words and a sophisticated accent, Billy?" Carly asked.

"He thinks he's Einstein," Sam joked, and playfully ruffled Billy's hair.

"It's quite entertaining to speak like this," Billy grinned as they walked over to a large table near the man. "And it's great practice of vocabulary."

Suddenly, the bell to the entrance rang, causing the five kids and the man to look over. A short, stocky man with broad shoulders walked into the shop. After a quick order, he strolled past the kids with a steaming cup.

As he walked by them, Sam looked up at him and said in a deep voice, "Yo."

The man gave him a stern look, then brushed past them and went over to the man's table.

"So we didn't miss it," Jerry remarked quietly.

"I wish we had," Sam muttered. He turned on his cell phone, put earphones in his ears, and tilted his chair onto its two back legs, resting his legs on the table.

The two strangers began their conversation, with rough and indistinct talk. The kids were able to hear the one with the briefcase say, "You're late . . . I don't want to . . . excuses."

As they talked, every so often they would look over at the gang's table. When they did, Billy would do things like show the group his chain, and brag that it was made of solid gold.

The kids couldn't hear most of the men's talk, but at one time, they heard the stocky man say in a harsh voice, "They're in the caves . . . diamonds . . . keep them safe . . . DeWitt will do that."

"They mentioned jewels. Maybe they smuggled them from California!" Jerry exclaimed in a hoarse whisper.

"They acquired jewels," Billy corrected, pushing up his glasses. "That doesn't mean they stole them."

The kids continued talking to lessen any suspicion from the men.

"Man, those donuts were good!" Billy remarked. "I wonder if I have some more money. Hey Jack, I'll loan you my chain for $50.00!"

The kids laughed, then looked at the man.

". . . flight . . . several days . . . make sure . . . Lark . . .tomorrow . . . ."

After finishing their drinks, the men quickly exited through the back door of the bakery.

"Let's follow them!" Jerry said excitedly.

"Huh? What?" Sam jolted from his relaxed position.

The gang hurried outside, hopped on their bikes, and went to follow the men.

Minutes later, the gang saw the men turn into a cheap motel.

"That's probably where the stocky one's staying," Jerry watched, "and any others involved in the theft."

"Yeah, like you know they're thieves," Sam said sarcastically.

"I doubt it." Jack put his foot down to stop his bike. "If the men do have diamonds, why would they stay in a back-alley motel?"

"Because they wouldn't want to attract any attention," Jerry retorted.

"But the man with the briefcase is staying in a popular hotel," Jack shot back. "Our hotel, and he's a smuggler."

"We don't exactly know if he's a criminal," Billy mentioned.

Jack rolled his eyes.

"Let's not argue," Carly stopped the boys. "At least not right here. C'mon, it's time for dinner."

The kids hopped on their bikes and rode to the hotel.

# Chapter 6

"Hello, boys!" The receptionist greeted Jack and Billy with a smile. They had gotten to the hotel ahead of the others. "Your parents are in the food hall."

"Many thanks, mada—" Billy started, but Jack cut him off.

"We'll be going now."

Jack smiled at the clerk, then started nudging Billy toward the food hall. Jack then muttered,

"No sophisticated accents in front of people, okay?"

The boys laughed as they entered the food hall. But they suddenly froze in their tracks. The man with the briefcase was helping himself to macaroni and cheese!

"How did he get here so fast?" Jack stared, awestruck at the appearance of the man.

"The most probable conclusion would be a taxi," Billy said quietly.

"L-let's go get some food."

The man was talking to a woman who wanted to see how the mac and cheese was. The boys grabbed plates, grabbed some food, and walked back to their parents.

"Where were you?" Dad demanded gruffly, but the twinkle in his eyes gave away that he was trying not to laugh.

"Sorry, boss," Jack tried to growl in a raspy voice with food in his mouth. "Me and the gang

would have gotten here sooner, but you know about the traffic issues.”

They both laughed, and Mom asked, “Did you get enough veggies? I don’t want you eating just meat.”

“Mom, half my plate is veggies, of course it’s mixed in with the fried rice and shrimp.”

They laughed again, and continued to chat while they ate.

“But really, where were you all?”

“We were just. . .riding around,” Jack answered, trying to avoid the question. “Lost track of time a little bit.”

Mom raised her eyebrows, but didn’t question.

When they finished dinner, the kids headed to Billy and his family’s room to do some research.

“Let’s start with the news,” Jerry suggested.

Billy flipped open his laptop, and soon found several articles about a bank robbery that had

recently taken place a few blocks down from the hotel where they were staying.

"The robbery was done by three men," Billy said, quickly reviewing the facts. "$40,000 was stolen. A pedestrian claimed to see the robbers come out of the building with large bags and hurry into a blue car."

"The man with the briefcase could be connected!" Jack jumped up excitedly as he read.

Billy pushed up his glasses as he turned to Jack. "The report says it happened last night."

"Then the man came to pick up the loot, not rob the bank."

"It would be a good plan to transport the money," Jerry and Carly agreed.

"But he doesn't even have a car," Billy mentioned, "or he wouldn't need to ride in a taxi. And I thought you said he was working with smugglers."

"He could be working with both some other way then," Jack argued. "He'll get paid by both groups, then sneak out of the country so he doesn't get caught."

"Guys, we shouldn't argue." Sam tried to calm Jack and Billy.

"Why would he leave the country?" Billy kept going. "He could just move to a different state, change names and clear up his record."

"So he doesn't leave the country. He still could be working with both."

"Now you're just jumping to conclusions."

Each idea Jack proposed, Billy quickly shot down, until finally Billy's mother came into the room.

"It's time to recharge," she said to them.

The kids groaned.

"But, Mom, we're doing important research." Billy spun around in the rolling chair, and his glasses flew off his face.

"You all need at least ten hours of sleep in order to properly function. Now it's time for bed." Mrs. Jones picked up the glasses and handed them to Billy. He grinned sheepishly.

Jerry, Jack and Carly went back to their rooms.

In Jack's room, his mom was using her laptop. "Mom, can I say goodnight to Carly and her family?" he asked.

"Sure, but be quick."

After exchanging goodnights, Jack went back to his room and went to sleep.

The next day, Jack woke up from a startling dream about the man with the briefcase and the gang.

Jack's head swarmed with questions about the meeting. *Who are DeWitt and Lark? Where are they keeping the stolen jewels? And where are the smugglers going to be for their next meeting?* He

shook his head. Right now, he needed a good breakfast.

Jack jumped out of bed and opened the door just as a large family of seven walked by. Two of the girls giggled, but the rest of the family pretended not to notice. Embarrassed, Jack quickly closed the door. He had forgotten to change out of his pajamas!

Jack changed into jeans and a t-shirt, and headed to the food hall for breakfast. When he got there, the Hankerson family, the Jones family, and the Smith family along with his parents were all eating and talking.

Billy noticed Jack. "Jack, the breakfast here is extraordinary!"

"Extraordinary as in good or as in bad?" Jack asked.

"It's astounding! Brilliant! Magnificent!"

"Great," Jack replied, "but no more speaking like that. I have a hard time understanding what you're saying."

Jack grabbed a plate, filled it with pancakes, sausage, and eggs, and sat down. After taking a few bites he remarked, "Wow, this *is* good!"

Carly walked over with her empty plate. "Hi, Jack! What do you think about the food?"

"It's really good."

"An astoundingly genius meal!" Billy took his last bite and sighed in satisfaction.

Carly laughed, then went to the food tables. But he soon returned with her plate still empty.

"Excuse me," she said to the waitress who came to their tables, "do you know what happened to the sausage?"

"If it's not there, then there's no more currently." She quickly filled the empty glasses with orange juice, then left their table.

Billy said in mock despair, "I admit, I ate the last of the delicious food. I ate the delicacy with regret and swallowed the splendid sausage in sorrow. My apologies, young lass. I suppose they will produce more of the sausage in a matter of minutes."

"It's okay," Carly told him, "but why are you using those big words?"

"I told you children the other day that it was entertaining to speak in this manner, but you must have not paid any attention, dear boy."

Carly frowned playfully.

"By the way," Billy changed the subject, "I was doing some research this morning and I came across reports of a theft at a local jewelry shop, either last night or early this morning. $8,000 worth of rings, necklaces, bracelets, and other jewels were stolen. Apparently, whoever pulled that crime left some clues."

"What clues?" all the kids leaned forward.

"For starters, they were in view of the security cameras. I made a quick visit to the crime scene today and—"

"You went to the shop?" Carly interrupted. "How early do you wake up?"

"Always at sunrise," Billy shrugged nonchalantly. "But like I was saying, I visited the scene and the owner allowed me to watch the footage. It appeared to be a one-man job, since only one person was seen on the video. The one set of footprints at the back door might have confirmed it. After some research, it turned out to be a size 11 boot print."

"So, the man with the briefcase stole some jewelry early this morning for himself?" Jack asked.

"You can't pin everything on him. Besides, from the video footage, he's too tall to be the thief. There were no fingerprints in the shop, so the

robber must have worn gloves. The thief also broke the lock on the back door."

"You're taking this case pretty seriously," Carly said. "Maybe too seriously."

After breakfast, Jack told his parents about their plans for the day. At least, he told them, "We're heading out to do some more sight-seeing."

"Be back at the hotel by 12:30," his mom answered. "We'll be going to the first event of your father's class reunion."

"Ok."

Jack went back to his room, grabbed his backpack, and headed for the door. While he waited outside for the rest of the kids, he saw the man with the briefcase walk into the food hall.

He grabbed a plate and loaded it with eggs. When he got to a table and sat down, he started moving the eggs around with his spoon, then he

tilted it toward the window. Jack looked at the window for a second and saw a figure peer into the hotel and look around.

At that moment, Carly walked in with her satchel. Jack immediately radioed Carly. "Carly, the man with the briefcase is doing something with his plate! Take a photo of it and him!"

Carly's walkie-talkie was on the loudest setting possible, so everyone looked over at her, including the man. For a split second, Carly hesitated, but soon had her camera in her hand. She snapped a picture of the man before he could hide his plate. The man roared in anger, threw his plate into the trash, and ran out of the hotel. Carly raced out after him.

"I got the photo!" she called to Jack. "Get the others!"

"But where will we find him?" Jack asked, running after Carly.

"I think he's heading to the nearest taxi stop two blocks down the street in his direction. Meet me there! And make it quick!"

Jack sprinted back into the hotel, where Billy, Sam, and Jerry had just walked downstairs. "C'mon guys," he called to them. "Hurry!"

He rushed back out, unchained all their bikes, and hopped on his without waiting for the rest of the gang.

The other boys soon caught up to him.

"Where are we going?" Jerry asked.

"After the man with the briefcase." Jack pedaled madly.

"All of this extreme physical activity is burning me out!" Billy panted.

Sam was already ahead of them. He crossed the street and sped down the hill. When he got to the taxi stop, he saw Carly in a struggle with the man. Sam slid his bike into the grass and hopped off.

"What's the bright idea?" the man snarled at Sam and Carly. "Can't a man hail a taxi?"

"Not when you're a criminal!" Carly blurted.

The man's eyes widened. "I don't know what you're talking about. I'm not a criminal. I'm a lawyer."

"What?" Jack, Billy, and Jerry had just arrived.

The man with the briefcase stuck a hand into his jacket and withdrew a business card. He handed it to Carly. "My name's Theodore Simpson. I work at Wallace and Garner Law Firm."

Mr. Simpson's name was on the card, as well as the firm. On the corner of the card was a diamond, the same mark as on his briefcase.

Jack wasn't ready to give up. "Then why were you at Lily's Bakery yesterday?"

Mr. Simpson glared at him. "I was meeting with a client."

"Who are Lark and DeWitt?"

The lawyer's face reddened, but he replied calmly, "Lark is my client's brother. DeWitt is a lawyer friend of mine who's helping on this case."

Jack, Carly, Billy, and Jerry looked at each other, red-faced and embarrassed.

"I'm very sorry, sir," Sam apologized. "I tried to stop them, but they wouldn't listen." Sam gave the kids a stern look.

"It better not happen again," Mr. Simpson said sharply. A taxi pulled up at the stop just then, and the man got in, shutting the door behind him.

"I can't believe you guys actually thought he was a smuggler," Sam said angrily as they walked back to the hotel. The kids were too ashamed to ride their bikes.

"We made a mistake, ok?" Jack retorted, shoving his hands into his pockets.

"A big one," Carly admitted.

Billy stared at the sidewalk. "I feel chagrined."

"What's chagrined?" Carly asked.

"Distressed or humiliated. Or sometimes both."

"Ah."

"Look on the bright side," Jerry said, trying to cheer up the would-be detectives. "We solved the mystery, just not in the way we hoped."

"Yeah, right," Jack muttered.

After their encounter, the gang went with their parents to the first event of their fathers' class reunion. They took the bus to their old college campus. There, they walked to the administration building and were led to a large room filled with people.

Jack's parents soon fitted into the group, leaving Jack and his friends sitting at a table close to the exit.

"What do we do now?" Jerry asked.

Carly glanced at the food table. "Ooh! They have taquitos! Sorry guys, but I'll see you later." Carly dashed away, her love of food overcoming her urge to stay with her friends.

Jack soon also became interested in the reunion and left the table to talk to the children of other parents.

Sam got bored the moment they entered the room, and was already scrolling on his phone, his earphones in tight.

A while later, Jerry put his head in his hands. "I'm bored."

"Same here." Billy pushed up his glasses.

Every once in a while, someone would come to their table and say hi. Sam would look up from his phone and force a smile, while Jerry and Billy politely engaged in a small conversation.

After a woman left their table, Jerry stood to his feet. "I saw a vending machine down the hall," he said to Billy. "I'll be right back."

Jerry then left the room. As he walked down the hall, he passed a classroom. The door was slightly open, and voices were arguing.

"I don't want any excuses, Hank!" a voice shouted. "We're going to get the job done, with or without your help."

"I'll do better next time."

"There won't be a next time. You understand?"

Jerry heard footsteps heading for the door, so he hid inside the next classroom. He peeked his head out of the room and saw a short man walk briskly down the hallway. *That might be Hank, Jerry thought. I should follow him, just to see what they're up to.*

When the man turned a corner, Jerry followed him. The man walked downstairs through a dark auditorium. Jerry started to follow, but soon tripped over a chair leg. The short man looked over his shoulder. When he saw Jerry, he

quickened his pace and exited through a side door. Jerry leaped to his feet and hurried after him. But when he got to the door, the short man was gone.

Disappointed, Jerry walked back upstairs to the vending machine. When he got three bags of chips, he headed back to the reunion. Billy and Sam were still sitting in their chairs.

"What took you so long?" Billy asked.

Jerry handed him a bag of chips. "I was walking down the hall when I heard people talking. One of the classrooms was slightly open, and two people were arguing. I didn't hear much, but I did see a short man walk out. When I tried to follow him, he noticed me and got away. The man looked like the one at the bakery with Mr. Simpson."

"Do you think it was just a coincidence?" Billy asked.

"Maybe. I did hear one of them talking about getting a job done. It might just be that I'm anxious to solve a mystery, but the conversation sounded pretty suspicious." Jerry gave Sam a chip bag, who nodded in gratitude.

"Did you try to get a look at the other man?" Billy asked.

"No." Jerry jumped to his feet. "Maybe they're still there."

"Don't tell me you're back to spying on that guy," Sam said. "Didn't he explain everything to you? He's not a crook."

"Then what was the egg thing at breakfast for?" Jerry asked.

He and Billy hurried back to the classroom. This time the door was shut. Jerry put his ear to the door. He didn't hear anything, so he slowly opened the door. There were a few rows of desks in the middle of the room. A larger desk sat at the front of the room.

Billy felt the cushions of each chair. Two were warm. "I'm going to make an educated guess that two people were in here," he said to Jerry.

The boys searched the room but didn't find any more clues. Finally, they gave up and went back to the reunion.

"It looks like the party's over," Jerry said, noticing the people grabbing their purses and bags. "But let's not tell Jack and Carly about our finding just yet."

Billy nodded.

Jack and Carly walked over to the boys.

"Hey guys." Carly smiled with a taco in her hand. "Wasn't that a great reunion?"

"If you say so," Sam muttered, stuffing his phone into his pocket.

"We got to meet a bunch of Dad's classmates and their children," Jack said. "One boy could juggle six pencils!"

"Wow," Jerry said sarcastically.

Jack didn't hear him, so he kept talking.

Soon, the kids' parents were ready to leave, and they all took a bus back to Rosedale Hotel.

Inside their room, Jack watched his mom wrap a framed picture.

"Who's the present for?" Jack asked.

"An old college mate of mine. His name is Theodore Simpson. He and I graduated here in Chicago. After graduation, I moved to Michigan, but he stayed here and joined a law firm."

"I know. Me and the others met him this morning."

Mom looked puzzled. "Are you sure?"

"Yep. He was at the taxi stop."

"He couldn't have been there. He's in the hospital."

# Chapter 7

Jack raced out the room and into the Hankersons', where Carly, Billy, and Jerry were playing a board game.

"Guys, the man with the briefcase isn't Theodore Simpson!"

"What?" they all looked up.

"Mom said Mr. Simpson is in the hospital. The man with the briefcase was lying to us!"

"But we won't be able to find him anyway," Jerry said. "We don't know where he went."

"Why don't we go to the taxi stop and see if the driver is there," Billy suggested. "He could tell us where the stranger went."

"Aw, man," Carly groaned. "I just got Park Place."

The kids hurried outside to the taxi stop. Fortunately, the driver had just pulled up.

"Excuse me," Jack asked, "What was the address you drove the man with the briefcase to?"

"Why do you need that?" the driver answered.

"He might be a criminal!" Carly blurted.

The boys glared at her.

"Or the actor of a popular criminal in a movie," Carly said, blushing.

The driver scribbled the address on a piece of paper and handed it out the window. "If he's a

famous actor, tell the media I drove him places,"
he said with a smile.

As the gang walked away, Jerry asked,
"Should we go to the place?"

"We can try," Billy said. He quickly pulled up
the address on his smartwatch. "It's only a few
blocks away from the hotel."

"Then let's go!" Jack and Carly raced back to
the hotel to grab their bikes.


"Here we are." Jack looked up at a small
house with an overgrown lawn.

The kids walked up the porch steps. Jerry
knocked on the door. Almost immediately, a tall,
slim man opened the door.

"What do you want?" he asked sharply.

"Good evening, sir," Billy spoke up when no
one answered. "We were wondering, uh, if a man
with a diamond marked briefcase came here."

The man eyed them carefully. "Yeah. What of it?"

"We were just wondering. Thank you for your time."

The gang walked down the porch steps, leaving the man staring after them.

"What was that?" Jack asked Billy once they were out of earshot of the man.

"What was I supposed to tell him? That we were detectives trying to locate him?"

"Speaking of finding him," Carly said, "he might be back at the hotel now."

"You guys go ahead," Jerry said. "Billy and I will go to the motel and check on the short man."

Jack and Carly rode back to Rosedale Hotel. They walked upstairs to the man with the briefcase's room. He was on a phone call.

"I knew that decoy wouldn't last forever. I'll try something else. . .No, we'll continue with the

plan. I have an idea. Go get Lark. He's at the taxi stop by the hotel."

The man with the briefcase opened the door. Jack and Carly pretended to be deep in a conversation about cameras.

"So you're saying that the film in the SRD-30 is different than the film in the SRD-29?" Jack asked, faking curiosity.

"Yep," Carly said, actually engaged in the conversation. "I think it's kelp-based."

"Ok." Jack paused. *"What?"*

The man walked past them and started down the stairs.

"Let's follow him," Jack whispered to Carly.

He and Carly quietly walked downstairs. But the man with the briefcase was nowhere in sight.

"He must be outside," Jack said.

He and Carly raced outside. The man with the briefcase was walking down the street. Jack and Carly hurried after him. He turned a corner.

Jack quickly texted the other boys, telling them about the man with the briefcase, then he and Carly followed the man around the corner. The stranger walked briskly down the sidewalk.

As Jack and Carly followed him, they were surprised from behind. Sacks were thrown over their heads. They struggled as they were dragged a short distance and sat on the ground. Something was shoved into Jack's hand.

When the struggle was over, Jack and Carly took off the sacks and looked around. They were sitting against a brick wall in a dark alley. Jack looked at what was in his hand. It was a paper with a red diamond crudely sketched. Under it was the word, "Danger."

Carly leaned over and looked at the paper. Her heart raced as soon as she saw the single word. "I t-think it's a t-threat."

"Yeah, and do you see the diamond?" Jack pointed with a shaky hand. "It looks just like the one on the stranger's briefcase."

"We should tell the others."

The kids left the alley. As they walked back to the hotel, Jack called the other boys.

"This is getting dangerous," Billy said after hearing about the kids' encounter. "I think we should apprise the law enforcement."

"What's apprise?" Carly asked.

"To inform someone. In this case, inform the police."

"Ah."

"Yeah, that's a great idea," Sam agreed. "It's about time you all stop this 'investigation,' and turn it over to the police."

"No!" Jack blurted.

# Chapter 8

## (the day before)

The leaves on a lone tree fluttered as a heavy wind blew through a large backyard in Westport. It was a cold day, despite being the beginning of summer. A boy opened the back door of his house and walked across the yard. He pulled his jacket closer to his shivering body as he trudged through the grass.

As he climbed the tree into a treehouse, another club member was there to greet him.

"Hi, Mike." A tall, slender girl with dark hair stuck her head out of the treehouse window.

"Hey Rachel. Where's Robby?"

"He's cleaning out the closet," she replied.

Robby was a thick, stocky boy similar in build to Jerry. He was sitting on a stool stacking papers in front of a closet with a broom leaning on the door.

Mike walked to the back of the structure. "Hey Robby."

"Hi, Mike." Robby started to turn around, but as he turned, he bumped into the door. The broom fell forward, aiming at Mike. Mike jumped to the side, allowing the broom to fall right beside him.

"Sorry about that." Robby grinned sheepishly.

"No problem." Mike picked up the broom and moved it over. "Have you fully recovered from the flu?"

"Yep. My mom finally allowed me to go outside today." Robby handed him a bundle of papers. "Here are some speeches Jack made last year."

"I can't believe we still have them." Mike read through some of them quickly.

"Hey, let's contact the others in Chicago," Robby suggested. "We haven't heard from them in a few days."

"Good idea," Mike agreed. He called Jack on his smartwatch.

"Hello?" Jack answered.

"Hi," Mike said. "Are the others with you?"

"Just Carly right now."

"How are you liking your vacation?" Robby asked.

"It's great!" Carly said. "We've been having a lot of fun here. Lots of things to do."

"Of course, we're still working on the mystery," Jack said. He filled them in on what they had learned.

"Wow," Mike said when Jack finished. "Sounds like a tough one. Be careful out there. You never know what could go wrong. One time, I—"

"We'll be careful," Jack interrupted hastily, not in the mood for Mike's stories. "But we're kind of stuck. Any ideas?"

"Maybe search the Internet for that diamond mark on his briefcase," Robby suggested.

"Guys, come look out the window!" Rachel called out in an alarmed voice.

Mike and Robby rushed over. Four kids had entered the backyard and were marching toward the treehouse.

"Oh, no," Mike groaned. "It's the E-Bikers."

The E-Bike Gang closed in, trapping Mike, Rachel, and Robby in the treehouse. They had

squirt guns, water balloons, and plenty of water bottles for extra ammo.

"Sorry, Jack, but we've got to go," Mike said quickly. "Bye." He ended the call before Jack could reply.

Robby and Rachel grabbed water balloons out of the closet, while Mike pulled up the hose.

"Give up and shut down the club!" shouted Emma, the leader of the rival gang, "or get soaked with water! We will drench this treehouse!"

"Never," Mike answered.

"Then we will force you to!"

"It's pretty cold today for a fight," Rachel remarked, trying to persuade the kids not to start a battle. "And, a big storm is passing through Westport tomorrow."

Emma ignored Rachel's comments and turned to her companions. "Attack! Storm the treehouse!"

The gang ran forward, spraying their squirt guns. Mike pointed the hose at Timmy and fired, saturating him with water. Robby threw down balloons from the tree, filling the backyard with water. Rachel raised the Motorbike Gang's flag in direct defiance to the enemy club.

In response, the E-Bike Gang sent water spraying wildly through the windows of the treehouse. They aimed carefully, drenching the furniture inside. As Mike sprayed the hose, Kevin snuck across the yard. When he got to the hose's water source, he turned the water off, cutting off Mike's weapon. Soon, the water stopped running to the hose, and the gang lost one of their best weapons.

Hours later, it was evening, and the E-Bike Gang had to go home for dinner.

"We'll be back!" Emma promised before leaving.

Mike went inside of his house, and asked, "Mom, can Robby and Rachel stay over for dinner?"

"If it's okay with their parents," she replied.

After two calls, the three children were seated at the table. Mrs. Michaels placed four steaming plates of meatloaf, mashed potatoes, and string beans on the dinner table.

After the meal, the E-Bike Gang was back. Armed with their squirt guns, and with permission from their parents and Mike's mother, they brought sleeping bags and a tent to the backyard.

"We're laying siege to the treehouse," Emma explained to the confused Motorbikers.

Soon, the battle was again at full speed with water raining from each side. At dark, the battle paused. Ellie stood guard while the rest of the gang slept. Ten minutes after she was stationed, Mike called an emergency meeting.

"We need to begin Operation Hurricane."

"Okay," Rachel agreed, "but how do we get to Billy's house without waking them up? Ellie's on guard." She handed hot chocolate to Robby and Mike

Mike snorted. "Ellie's moonbathing."

"Is that even a thing?" Rachel asked.

"It is for her. You know, instead of sunbathing, she's—"

"We get it."

"I'm just saying."

"We could hop the fence," Robby suggested. "Two of us will sneak out, while the other stays on guard."

"I'll stay," Rachel offered.

"Fine with us," Mike and Robby accepted.

As the boys crept through Mike's yard, Ellie was awakened by the hoot from an owl. She looked around. Mike and Robby froze in their positions. After a minute, Ellie dozed back off to sleep. The two boys leaped over the fence, walked

around to the front of Mike's house, and grabbed their motorbikes. They crept to the end of the block before getting on and speeding down the street.

Soon, they were at Billy's garage. They opened the side door, which was always unlocked, and walked into the garage. Two cars were parked inside. Underneath a table near the wall sat a large box that read, "Property of William E. Jones."

All sorts of drills, bits, and soldering irons were on and hanging above the table. The boys opened the box. Inside, a large metal contraption with ten hose-like openings sat on a big set of wheels.

Mike and Robby closed the box and lifted the Gardenator 3000. They struggled to carry it out of the garage, through the side door, and onto Robby's trailer. They hopped back onto their

bikes and rode off, being careful not to make their turns too sharp.

When they got back to the house, the E-Bike gang had woken up. Loud laughter could be heard from inside the tent. Ellie was now inside the tent, and Timmy was outside on guard with his squirt gun. After a few minutes, he laid down on his sleeping bag, rolled over, and went to sleep. Robby and Mike brought out Billy's invention without him knowing.

The boys tiptoed across the yard to the treehouse (at least as much as they could carrying the heavy box) and put the invention into a wooden crate. A pulley system connected the crate to the treehouse. Mike and Robby climbed up into the treehouse and lifted the contraption up to them.

Mike tapped Rachel on the shoulder and said, "We have the Gardenator 3000."

After the box was safely stored out of reach of enemy fire, they discussed their next plan.

"Soon, our enemies will be asleep," Mike said, "and then we can raid their supplies."

After a few hours of sleep, Robby woke up. He awakened the others, and then they set to work. Mike took a flashlight out of the closet, and handed it to Rachel.

"Flash this if Timmy wakes up," he instructed her.

Mike then handed Robby a large bucket.

"Take as many of their water balloons and extra ammo as possible."

Robby nodded.

Mike took an armload of water balloons for himself and left the treehouse. He snuck into the tent with the sleeping E-Bikers, and placed a few water balloons inside their sleeping bags.

"This ought to wake them up," he chuckled.

Robby snuck behind Timmy and the tents. He grabbed the balloon stash and stuck half of it into his bucket. He also stuck several of the water bottles into his pockets, then ran back to the treehouse.

Mike snuck a couple of balloons into Timmy's sleeping bag, then he also left.

When the boys got back to their base, they crowded at the window to watch the reaction. After ten minutes, which to them felt like an eternity, they were rewarded for their work. The sound of splashes, screams, and shouts came out of the tent.

"WHO PUT WATER BALLOONS IN HERE?" Emma screamed.

"The Motorbikers most likely," said Kevin.

"I'm soaked!" Ellie wailed.

Soon, Timmy woke up from the spray of the water balloons, and dragged his sleeping bag into

the tent. "Someone put water balloons in my sleeping bag!" he growled.

"It was the Motorbikers!" Emma responded.

She immediately started an emergency meeting.

"What should we do?" asked Kevin.

"Fight them!" Emma squished a water balloon with one hand.

They all cheered and started spreading suggestions.

"We can use our stash behind the tents."

"We can sneak into their treehouse."

Filled with rage, Emma grabbed another water balloon and threw it at the Motorbike Gang's flag. It missed, and sailed over the fence into a neighboring yard.

"They even stole half of our ammo!" she roared. "Attack, E-Bikers! ATTACK THE MOTORBIKE GANG!"

Her voice echoed into the night sky.

The gang grabbed their squirt guns, filled them with what was left of their ammo, and began spraying the insides of the treehouse.

"Take cover!" Mike called to his companions.

They ducked behind the podium as water drenched the house. Rachel brought down Billy's invention and rolled it in front of the treehouse. The enemy sprayed water on her the entire time. Rachel climbed back into the treehouse soaking wet. Mike grabbed the remote to the Gardenator 3000, and pressed the on button.

Immediately, it began turning. The invention picked up speed rapidly, shooting water in every direction. The E-Bike Gang tried taking cover behind their tent, but the force of the spray threw it around the backyard.

"Retreat!" Emma cried. "Retreat!"

They ran, dropping their guns and hopping onto their bikes in the driveway. They pedaled hard, trying not to waste time getting out of there.

Mike, Robby, and Rachel looked up. The flag, though torn, ripped, and wet, was still fluttering in the early morning breeze. They cheered, celebrating a major victory for the gang.

Just then, Mrs. Michaels opened the back door. "What is all that racket this early in the morning?"

"Nothing much," Robby replied. "Just a victory for the Motorbike Gang."

The three kids laughed.

As they were cleaning up the yard, Rachel asked, "Should we return their tents and guns?"

The three laughed again.

# Chapter 9

Jack quickly turned around, making sure no one heard him.

"We are not going to tell the police," he said again more quietly. "We're close to solving the case!"

"But, we won't be able to prevent the men from plundering banks and ransacking jewel shops across Chicago," Billy argued in his sophisticated accent. "That is, if they are even thieves."

Jack wasn't paying attention, and he had accidentally turned up the volume on his watch. Billy's voice thundered across the sidewalk.

Jack heard Billy's objection loud and clear, which upset him for the moment. As he and Carly walked back to the hotel, a blue Mustang drove past him down the street. Jack estimated it was going at least 50 MPH since it looked like the car was passing the speed limit.

The driver threw a paper tied to a rock out of the car next to a trash can by Jack and Carly.

When he noticed the kids, the man tried to yell over the roaring car, "Get outta here, kids!"

Jack ran to the trash can. *I hope no one sees me,* he thought.

He pulled out the paper and it read,

Myles, this is Lark. DeWitt has the merchandise safely out of sight. All we need now is to silence the Wesley kid for good. I'll do that.

"Guys are you still here?" Jack asked.

"Yeah."

"I just read a message from the smugglers. They're out to get me!"

"Who's on the paper?" Carly asked, leaning forward to look at the note.

"DeWitt, Lark, and Myles. But I don't know who Myles is though."

"He's another member of the gang, obviously," Jerry replied.

"Jerry and I are on our way back from the motel," Billy said. "The short man, who we think is named Hank, just got picked up by a Blue Mustang. It's too fast for us to follow, so we're heading back to the hotel."

"That's the car that just passed us!" Jack said. "The driver threw this message out of the window."

"Guys, I just thought of something," Carly said. "This message couldn't have been from Lark. The man with the briefcase told someone to pick him up at the taxi stop! And that was just a few minutes ago."

"So then this message is a fake!" Billy realized.

"Who's closest to the taxi stop?" asked Jack in excitement.

"I think we are," Carly said.

"Then you'll need to hold off Hank until the rest of us get there," Billy said.

"Wait," Jerry said, "They can't go by themselves. They'll get beaten up. Hank and Lark are criminals, remember?"

"For the last time, we don't know that!" Sam shouted angrily. "All this spying and fighting and

trailing over a bunch of nonsense. And I have to take the brunt of it.”

“Since Sam’s still at the hotel,” Billy said, ignoring his brother’s remarks, “he’s closest to the taxi stop. Sam, you can go with Jack and Carly and hold off the men until we arrive.”

“Why am I always the one babysitting?” Sam retorted. “I should get paid for this.”

“We need to hurry though,” Jerry said, trying not to laugh at Sam’s comments. “It’s about time for us to head to the hotel for dinner.”

“Ok,” Jack replied. “We’re on our way. Jack and Carly out.”

Jack and Carly ran as fast as they could to the taxi stop. Sam was able to get to the stop just before them, who were down the block. A blue Mustang was parked at the curb. A very tall man was standing next to it, talking to a man whose head stuck partly out of the passenger window.

“Hey, stop!” Sam yelled.

The man in the car looked over, and saw Sam. "That's one of the Wesley kid's pals. We gotta move!"

Sam jumped off his bike and ran to confront the tall man. "Hey, what's the rush?"

Jack and Carly raced in and blocked the man from entering the car. Jack slammed the door closed.

"Back off!" The passenger door opened, and a short man emerged from the car. It was Hank.

Jack looked at the tall man. He looked like the man they had met earlier.

"What's the deal with the phony lawyer business?" Carly asked.

Hank stared at him. Suddenly, he shoved Jack into Sam and leaped back into the Mustang. "Let's get outta here!"

The tall man ripped open the rear door of the car and hopped in. The car sped away from the curb before the man could even close the door.

Carly grabbed the camera out of her satchel, and took three photos of the car. It roared past a red light, triggering a series of honking cars. Carly put the camera back into her bag and joined Jack and Sam.

"Did you see the look on Hank's face when we asked him about the fake identity?" Jack asked. "I'm sure they're doing illegal stuff."

"I agree," Carly answered.

"Tracking criminals is a job for the police," Sam said. "If they are crooks, we'll leave it to the police to capture them."

Jack and Carly groaned. Carly called Billy and Jerry on her watch and told them what happened at the taxi stop.

"I agree with your hypothesis about the men," Billy said.

"The Mustang picked up Hank and Lark," Jerry said. "Including the driver, there are three people riding in the car."

"And if they're all headed to the same place, that means they're up to something," Jack said. "We should find out, then get our bikes and follow them, and then ram into the criminals' car while they're driving in it!"

Jack was getting a little too impulsive.

"Calm down, Jack," Sam said. "We don't even know if they're criminals."

"Remember," Billy corrected Jack, "no unnecessary combat."

"We need to get back to the hotel," Carly said.

"You're right," Jerry replied. "We're almost there now. We'll see you when we get there. Jerry and Billy out."

When the gang got back to the hotel, Mrs. Wesley was waiting for them. "Where were you all?" she asked. "You were supposed to be here half an hour ago. Didn't you get my text messages?"

"Sorry, Mom," Jack replied, "But we were busting criminals!"

Mom laughed.

"Your dad is in the restroom," she said to him. "He'll be out soon."

Mrs. Wesley looked at them, and noticed their rough clothes. Concerned, she asked again, "But what really happened to you all?"

"We were busting criminals," Jack said again.

"Tell me the truth," Mom demanded. "Your joke isn't funny anymore."

"We were fighting crooks!" Jack cried for the third time.

He took a giant breath, then told the events that happened during the past two days. "We tried to stop one of them, who stays at this hotel, but he tricked us into thinking he was Theodore Simpson, then Jerry heard a suspicious conversation at the college yesterday, and saw a man the phony lawyer met with the day before

yesterday, then . . ." Jack decided to not mention the threat message, not wanting to worry his mother. ". . . then Sam, Carly, and I confronted a man involved with the bad guys at the taxi stop a minute ago, but he escaped in a blue car, and the driver was bad, too."

Mom gave him a stern look. "How long have you been doing this?"

Jack hesitated. "A little more than a week?"

Mom's face was red as she put two and two together. "Is that why you were late for dinner the day before school let out for the summer?"

Jack said nothing as his cheeks turned crimson. His mom had remembered!

"Jack Wesley, tell me where you had gone that day."

"Uh. . .to the airport. . .on a bus."

"Jack Wesley! You know you shouldn't be out after school without permission. And going to the airport by yourself?"

"Uh, Mrs. Wesley, I went with him." Carly looked at the floor.

If Jack's mom's face was red, it now turned purple. "Jack, you are banned from leaving the hotel without Sam. You don't get any more pocket money, and you will drop this investigation. Do you understand?"

Jack nodded, fighting back tears.

"If you really think those men are criminals, you should tell the police, not try to stop them yourselves. Now go upstairs and change your clothes for dinner."

She looked at the other boys. "You boys should let your parents know about the situation."

Jack sighed as he walked upstairs.

When he and the others changed, they went to the food hall.

"So, what should we do about this situation?" Jack asked when they sat at a table.

The others paused at hearing the note of anger in Jack's voice.

Billy hesitantly responded. "Alert the police department. We should notify a constable of this crisis forthwith."

"But, if Mom doesn't believe me, then the police won't either," Jack protested.

"We need to at the very least attempt to inform them, and if they don't believe us, then we'll have to take matters into our own hands."

"Whoa, didn't Jack just get in trouble for doing that?" Carly spoke up.

"Right," Jerry said. "I'm sure our parents will agree with Mrs. Wesley's decision and stop us from investigating."

"Do we all agree?" Jack looked over at the other boys.

"Yes," they replied.

"Okay, after we tell the others back home, we'll let the police know about these smugglers."

After dinner, Jack and his friends went to his room for a little while before bed. Jack sat silently at the window, taking in the view. He enjoyed viewing the big city whenever he could.

Jack looked down at the street. He saw a man with a black coat and sunglasses walking on the sidewalk. Before he was out of view of the window, he took off his glasses, and Jack caught a glimpse of his face. Jack wondered if he was the man with the briefcase. He brushed it off, thinking about his conversation with Mom.

Billy took the opportunity to try to connect with Mike, Rachel and Robby.

"There's quite a storm out here," Mike answered, "But we get your—" The connection was cut off by loud static.

Billy leaned over and tapped Jack's shoulder, snapping him out of a daydream.

"My correspondence with the trio was interrupted. I will begin attempting to reconnect with them immediately.

# Chapter 10

Jack and the families visited a museum that afternoon. They learned a lot during the trip about moments in history, saw cool artifacts, and enjoyed a presentation on ancient pyramids. Billy especially liked the exhibits about famous technological inventions.

Carly squealed when she saw an exhibit about cameras. "Look! It's one of the first SRD-1 models ever made!" She pointed to an old, dull gray camera.

"The camera that changed photographic technology forever," Billy said, moving closer to the camera

Jack groaned. "It's a camera."

"It's a dream come true to see such a revolutionary piece of history on display!" Carly said. "I wish I could take a photo of it."

A man in a black uniform stepped close to them. "No flash photography," he said unkindly.

"We know," Sam replied evenly, and the gang moved on away from the exhibit.

"As if we can't see the big signs all around the museum that say 'No Flash Photography,'" Sam muttered.

Jerry looked over his shoulder. The man in the uniform was scowling in their direction.

"I think he heard Sam," Jerry whispered to Billy.

Billy smiled.

The next day, the gang went to tell the police their suspicions about the men they had been following.

Jack couldn't wait. He burst through the police station door. "We need to speak to the chief immediately!"

"What's your hurry?" The secretary turned his head from a computer screen.

"There are crooks around! And they might have the jewels from California!"

There was a moment of silence, then the secretary burst into laughter.

Carly elbowed Jack. "They didn't say jewels from California!" she whispered.

Billy leaned over the front desk. "You've got to let us forewarn your superiors."

"Get out of here!" The man waved his hand as he chortled.

"But—"

The man walked out of the room to tell the others. Soon the entire building was filled with laughter.

"We have proof!" Jack shoved Jerry's voice recorder and the man with the briefcase's phony business card at the secretary. "A man we're suspicious of told us he was Theodore Simpson. But the real Mr. Simpson's in the hospital!"

"Do you know his name?"

"Uh, no."

The man shrugged, then called an officer over. He played the recording.

After hearing the talk at the bakery, the officer shrugged. "We'll try to pick up the man for questioning, but other than that there's not much we can do."

Jack moaned.

Billy scribbled the address of Rosedale Hotel on a piece of paper, as well as the man with the

briefcase's hotel room, then handed it to the officer.

"Let's leave." Carly opened the door disappointingly.

Sam and Jerry were waiting for them outside.

"That was quick." Sam looked at the dejected kids.

"They didn't really believe us," Carly muttered.

As the five walked back down the street, they discussed their next plan.

"We need to put a stop to those men," Jack said.

"But how?" asked Carly. "We don't even know what crime they're committing."

"And you got in trouble, so you can't," Sam added.

"Let's do a proper analysis of the facts we gathered so far," Billy suggested.

Suddenly, Jerry's stomach growled. "Can we do it at a pizzeria? I have a hankering for Chicago-style pizza."

The others laughed.

"Excellent proposition, Jerry." Billy smiled.

The gang visited Tony's Pizza Shack for lunch. When they walked inside, a lanky teenager stood at the counter. A nametag on his shirt read "Logan."

"Welcome to Tony's," Logan greeted them blandly. "Today's Discount Wednesday. All pizza sizes are 25% off."

"What are we going to get?" Jack asked the others.

Billy stared intently at the menu. "I want to make sure we get the most out of our capital."

"Capital?" Carly asked.

"It's another word for money."

"Ah."

But after a minute, Billy was still looking at the menu.

"Come on," Jack groaned. "Hurry up. We need to get to work on the case."

Logan looked quizzically at Sam.

"They're trying to solve a 'crime,'" Sam explained.

Billy finally ordered a medium sized pizza. The kids went to a table and started discussing the case. Carly pulled out printed copies of the photos she had taken during the past few days.

Jack picked up a picture of the suspects' blue car. "The license plate number of the Mustang is WXH-1244."

"The names of the men are Hank, Lark, DeWitt, and Myles." Carly wrote down the information on a notepad. "But we don't know the name of the man with the briefcase."

"The picture he made on his plate looks like a diamond," Jack noticed. "It looks like the mark on

his briefcase, the phony business card, and the warning the masked men gave us."

"Could he have meant their jewels in the message?" Carly asked.

"And who did he show the message to?" Jerry asked.

"The mark could possibly be a signal," Billy said, "referring to—"

"A robbery!" Jack interrupted excitedly. "Like the one that happened several days ago."

"I was going to say a meeting or secret messages."

"Jack might be right," Carly said. "If they are planning a robbery, that would explain the last few meetings, including the ones we haven't been to."

"That's very unlikely," Billy objected. "First, if the symbol did mean a robbery, why would someone use it to threaten you? Second, the mark on his briefcase looks worn, as if it was there for more than just a week. Third—"

"Ok, ok," Jack interrupted. "It probably doesn't mean a robbery."

"Then what does it mean?" Jerry asked.

Jack looked over at Sam as he thought. Sam was talking to Logan about video games. The teenagers laughed at a joke Logan made.

Carly slumped in her chair. "This case is harder than I thought."

Billy looked at a few photos on the table. "The diamond mark on the man's briefcase and phony business card are colored blue. The mark on the danger message is red, and the message on the man's plate was technically yellow. Could the different colored marks mean different things?"

Carly sat up. "Maybe you're right."

Sam came over with the pizza. "Who's hungry?"

Jerry grabbed three slices before anyone else. "I sure am."

"We'll have to continue watching the man with the briefcase and his pals to get more clues," Jack said, grabbing a slice of pizza.

"That'll be harder now that they know we're on the case," Carly said.

When the gang got back to the hotel in the evening, their parents were already in the food hall. The kids went to their bathrooms and washed up. After their showers, they grabbed some food in the hall. After two plates of food and dessert, they walked to their rooms.

"Goodnight," Carly said to Jack. She yawned, then entered her room and closed the door.

Jack walked a few doors down to his room. He got into bed, turning his walkie-talkie on the lowest volume and placed it next to his pillow. *Just in case there's a bank robbery.* Pulling the blanket up to his chin, he closed his eyes and fell asleep.

The next morning, Jack met Jerry, Carly, and their parents in the food hall.

"Hello, Jack," Mr. and Mrs. Smith said, smiling.

"Hi," Jack replied as he walked past to sit down with Jerry and Carly at the next table.

"What took you so long?" Jerry grinned. "You were the one who woke me up."

Jack gave him a playful shove as he sat down.

In a few minutes, the Jones family and Jack's parents came into the hall.

When Billy and Sam got to the kids' table, Jerry asked, "What took you so long?"

Sam gave him a playful shove as they sat down.

"Hey guys, I think I see the man with the briefcase." Carly squinted to get a better look.

The other boys looked over. Sure enough, three tables away, the stranger with the briefcase was sitting with another man.

"Do you think that's one of the other smugglers?" Jerry asked.

"Most certainly." Billy pushed up his glasses. "At least, if they are smugglers. It might even be DeWitt or Myles, the two men we haven't seen yet."

After a few minutes of chatting, the men got up and left.

"Quickly, let's follow them," said Jack.

"No way." Sam looked up from his cell phone. "I haven't even finished my breakfast. And I'm planning on going to the arcade today."

The kids got up, put their dishes in a pile on the table, and speed-walked out of the building. Sam groaned, scarfed down the rest of his food, and followed reluctantly. When they all got outside, the man with the briefcase was on a phone call. The other man was already a block away.

"Guys, we need to follow him," Jack said as they stepped out of view.

"Wait," Carly reminded, "You can't investigate any more. And you can't even leave the hotel without Sam's supervision."

Jack sighed as he remembered.

"We could split up," Jerry suggested. "Jack—I mean, not Jack—Billy and Carly will watch the man with the briefcase. Sam and I will follow the other man."

The others agreed.

Sam rolled his eyes. "Whatever."

Jerry and Sam unchained their bikes and rode off. When they got to the end of the block, they turned and doubled back through an alley toward the man.

Jack went into the hotel while Billy and Carly watched their target. He looked as if he had been slapped in the face.

"Hurry up!" he said. "You and DeWitt need to move them to a safer place. You can't let anyone see you. We'll pick them up tomorrow morning."

There was a pause. "Fine, but make sure it's not the same one. And make sure to mark it."

The man hung up, and started walking back to the hotel. The kids stepped back into the building, trying their best to act casual. The man with the briefcase walked in. Billy sat in one of the chairs and grabbed a magazine to cover his face. Carly ran upstairs to hide.

The man with the briefcase walked up the stairs. Billy followed. The man walked into his room and shut the door quickly. Billy ran into his room, grabbed a glass, and rushed back into the hallway. He looked around. No one was there. He put the glass to the door and listened.

Carly crept out of the bathroom and put her ear to the door. They heard a radio and a few clicks. After several seconds, they heard a voice.

"Is that you, Wilson?"

"Yes," the man with the briefcase replied. "Get the plane ready. We'll be there tomorrow afternoon. Then, we'll leave the country and finish our deal. All that's left to do now is to collect the money and deal with the Wesley kid and his friends."

The two kids gasped.

"Are you sure you want to deal with those kids?" asked the person on the other end.

"Of course I do! They know too much. They even called the cops on me, and I got questioned by two officers. I'll have some of the others do the job. We'll see you tomorrow."

The radio turned off.

"Quickly, into my room!" Carly said. They ran, barely making it before Wilson opened the door.

"We need to apprise the others." Billy pushed up his glasses as he turned to Carly.

She agreed.

# Chapter 11

Jerry and Sam followed the stranger. The man walked to a car parked at the curb a few blocks away from the hotel, got in, and closed the door behind him. The car roared to life and pulled away from the curb. Jerry and Sam pedaled faster to keep up with it.

After several minutes, the car stopped in the small parking lot of a bank.

"Do you think he works here?" Jerry asked Sam.

Sam shrugged.

The man exited the vehicle and strode quickly into the bank. Jerry and Sam followed. Inside, the man walked around the front desk and passed a sign that read "Employees Only Beyond This Point."

"Excuse me," Jerry asked the lady at the front desk. "Do you know who the man that just came in here a few minutes ago is?"

"Frederick Clark," the woman answered. "He's the assistant branch manager of this bank."

"Thank you." Jerry and Sam walked out of the building.

"Now what?" Sam asked.

"I guess we can go back to the hotel now. But I'm getting suspicious. A bank branch manager working with criminals definitely means trouble."

"You don't even know if he's a criminal."

Jerry and Sam walked back to their bikes. But before they got on, the door to the bank opened. A tall man walked quickly out of the building.

"Frederick Clark again!" Jerry observed.

Clark hurried to his car and drove out of the parking lot. Jerry and Sam hopped back on their bicycles and followed him.

The car stopped at a tall apartment building a block away from the bank. Clark exited his car and walked in.

"Let's just get this over with," Sam said.

"I couldn't agree more." Jerry pedaled forward.

They parked their bikes at the bike rack close to the door. A car pulled up to the curb, but they didn't notice. The boys walked in.

A lanky teenager with wavy hair sat at the desk.

"How can I help you?" he grumbled, looking up from his phone and slurring his words a little.

"We're here to see someone," Jerry replied.

Jerry was a little worried the teenager wouldn't let him in. But the secretary just mumbled, "Whatever," and let them pass.

The boys turned and saw the bank branch manager walk briskly up the stairs. Sam and Jerry followed.

They made it to the 5th floor and watched as the man entered his room. They tiptoed to the door of the room and pressed their ears against it, trying to hear. They could hear the faint sound of a phone ringing.

As the boys listened, footsteps echoed through the hallway. A hand grabbed Sam's shoulder, and the boys spun around. Instantly, a fist slammed into Sam's face, sending him to the floor. Jerry looked up into the masked faces of two men. One was short, the other a heavy-set man with broad shoulders.

"Get the other one!" the short one snarled.

Jerry tried to make a run for it, but the big man grabbed him and pinned him to the wall.

"We're going on a little trip," the short one told him.

"You're Hank, aren't you?" Jerry boldly asked the short man, recognizing his voice.

The short man glared at him. "Why, yes, I am. But you can't prove nothin' if you try to go to the cops. Now get going!"

Hank shoved Jerry toward the stairs. The big man picked up Sam. During the walk, Hank muttered, "Look casual, or else!"

The men took off their masks when they reached downstairs. The big man had a wrinkled, tough-looking face. The other man was indeed Hank.

The men led the boys outside and into a blue Mustang parked at the curb.

"Get inside!" Hank ordered.

The boys complied. Suddenly, another masked figure inside the car pressed a cloth to their faces. Jerry and Sam blacked out.

When the boys woke up, they were inside a tiny dark room. The only light was coming through under the door.

"Boss says the job's almost done," said a masculine voice outside the room. "These came in the mail after weeks of waiting."

They heard a thump, and then a click.

"Finally," said another male voice, "our heaters."

"They have guns in there!" Sam whispered.

The men talked for a little while, then left the room.

"We're trapped," Jerry said.

After an hour, the boys heard the door open. Footsteps rang as someone entered the room.

"Time to get rid of those kids for good!" a voice chuckled.

"Get ready for a fight," Sam told Jerry as he balled up his fists.

The doorknob clicked as it unlocked, and the door swung open. Hank and the big man stood in the doorway.

Immediately, Sam swung a punch at the big man's face, catching him by surprise and sending him reeling into a chair behind him. Hank stepped forward to get at Sam, but Jerry kicked his shin, sending Hank sprawling to the floor.

The boys soon squirmed out of the fray, grabbed their phone and watch from off a desk by the front door, and dashed for the elevator. They pushed the first floor button, and the elevator closed before the men could get in.

The two boys met the men downstairs. They managed to slip past them and exit the building. The teenaged secretary watched them carelessly.

Jerry looked over his shoulder. He and Sam had just exited the motel that Hank was staying in. The two men burst through the door and continued their chase. As they ran, Jerry radioed the others.

"Guys, the men are chasing us!"

"Grab a taxi!" Billy quickly suggested. "They'll never attempt to attack you in public."

The boys flew to a nearby stop in time to hail a taxi.

"Rosedale Hotel, please!" they cried, jumping into the car.

The cab sped off right as the men turned the corner.

"We lost them," Jerry whispered.

After a few minutes, they reached the hotel.

"$6.50," said the driver.

"Who's paying?" Sam looked at Jerry.

"Not me," Jerry opened the door on his side and hurried out onto the sidewalk.

"Rock, paper, scissors is only fair," Sam said.

Jerry ended up winning.

Sam groaned, paid and thanked the driver, and exited the cab. The boys then walked into the hotel. Jack, Billy, and Carly were waiting at the door.

"You made it!" Carly sighed in relief.

"That was too close." Jerry bent over a chair in the lobby, gasping for breath.

"What happened to you?" Jack asked.

"We followed the man to a bank downtown and an apartment," Jerry said. "His name is Frederick Clark. He's the assistant branch manager of a bank several blocks away. When we got to the apartment, Hank and another man caught us. A third man knocked us out in their blue Mustang. When we woke up, we were locked in Hank's room at the motel. When they came back, we escaped."

Jack heard a car door close, and opened the lobby door. A sleek blue car roared away from the curb down the street.

Jack rushed back inside the hotel. "Guys, the Mustang just drove away!"

The other boys rushed outside just in time to see it make a turn a few blocks down the street.

"Did they follow us here?" Jerry asked.

"Maybe," Carly said, "but look!"

The boys turned toward the direction she was pointing. Two more bikes were parked at the bike rack.

"The men must have decided not to keep the bicycles," Billy said.

"Maybe they thought it would give them away or something," Jack said.

When the kids reentered the hotel, Jerry asked Jack, Carly, and Billy, "What did you learn?"

"The man with the briefcase is named Wilson," Billy told Jerry and Sam. "Whatever business they're conducting here is almost finished. Then they're going to pick up their bijoux—"

"What's bijoux?" Carly asked.

"It's the plural form of bijou, which means jewel or trinket."

"Ah."

"Anyway, the men are going to pick up their jewels tomorrow morning and take a flight out of the country in the afternoon to finish a deal they're involved in."

"If the men are dealing with jewels, then why did they need to come here?" Jack asked.

"Maybe they needed to meet with someone here," Carly suggested.

"This is one complicated mystery," Jerry said.

"Well, on the bright side," Billy said, "I had Rachel send me a package with some things we can use during sleuthing."

Billy showed them a small box.

"How did you get it so fast?" Jerry asked in amazement.

"My miniature hot air balloon." Billy pushed up his glasses triumphantly. "I had Rachel launch it this morning. I'm very delighted that it actually succeeded. Let's go to my room and I'll present them to you."

They hurried up the stairs into Billy's room. He opened the box.

"Ladies—er, lady—and gentlemen, these items will improve our investigation."

Billy pulled out pepper spray.

"These will be for defense. One for each of us."

Next, he took out a pair of goggles from the box. "These are night vision goggles. I made them

myself. We can use them if we ever need to do either early morning or late night sleuthing.”

“Which you most likely will not do,” Sam muttered.

Lastly, Billy pulled out flashlights. “You each can take one of these. I won’t need one, since I’ll be using the night vision goggles. You can brighten the light if needed for self-defense.”

“Great idea having Rachel send all this spy gear,” Jack said.

“I should have had her send some tracking devices,” Billy said, half-teasing and half-serious.

“I’m still not buying that they’re useful.”

“Now that all this spying stuff is over for now, can we finally go to the arcade?” Sam begged, being an avid fan of video games.

“Good idea,” the others agreed, except for Billy.

"You guys go ahead, I'll stay and do some internet research. Besides, someone needs to stay and watch the man with the briefcase."

"Okay," Jack said. "Meet us at the ice cream shop two blocks down from here in an hour."

"Sure."

Jack, Carly, Jerry, and Sam left the hotel, while Billy stayed back to work on a plan. On their way out, the man with the briefcase was in the food hall talking to one of the hotel staff members.

"Shh! The man with the briefcase is talking to a staff member!" Jerry said.

"Who cares?" Sam retorted.

They looked inside the room, and the man with the briefcase was coming right toward them! Quickly they ran down the hall before the man could spot them.

"Phew! That was close!" Carly said as they walked out the door. "But we need to hurry and

wrap up this case. The men are going to leave tomorrow.”

“We know.” Jack stuffed his hands in his pockets. “It’s just pretty challenging.”

# Chapter 12

Later that night, Jack awoke from his sleep to the sound of footsteps outside his door. Naturally, he got out of bed to investigate. Jack tiptoed to the door, not wanting to disturb his parents. He quietly opened the door and peeked out. Walking down the stairs was the man with the briefcase!

Jack followed him at a distance. When the man got downstairs, Jack stayed hidden on the staircase. The man with the briefcase strode to the door. Jack hurried back up the stairs to his room and looked out the window facing the street. A blue car pulled away from the curb and sped down away.

Immediately, Jack hurried back to his bed and grabbed his walkie-talkie. "Guys," he whispered hoarsely, "the man with the briefcase just got picked up by the Mustang!"

Jack then quickly changed his clothes and opened the door. The others were waiting in the hall. He had been the last one ready, even though it had only taken him 32 seconds to get his things and change. Even Carly had gotten ready before him.

"Next time," Billy shook his head, "try to be out in under 20 seconds."

Jack grimaced.

"There won't be a next time," Sam said. "We're never doing this again. I don't even know why I'm going with you guys."

"If you don't go, I can't go," Jack replied

"It's very caring of you," Jerry joked.

"And you're very funny," Sam said sarcastically

The gang crept down the stairs. They paused at the bottom, then ducked past the receptionist.

When they got outside, Carly asked, "How do we know where they're going?"

"Which way were they headed?" Jerry asked excitedly.

Jack pointed to the hotel's left.

"That's the way Frederick Clark took yesterday! It leads to the bank he works at."

"And if he's working with the men," Billy caught on, "they might just be robbing the bank right now!"

Billy ripped off his backpack. He opened it, took out a folder, and handed it to Jack. "Show the photos and clues we've gathered to the police.

Tell them about Frederick Clark. Then get to the bank."

"Aw, man," Jack moaned, "I have to do the boring job."

"You're not supposed to be investigating, remember?"

"Catching criminals isn't investigating. And, by going to the bank, I'll be supervised by Sam, just like my mom ordered."

"Don't try to weave around Mrs. Wesley's rules. You know there'll be consequences for sneaking out here anyway. Just go to the police."

"Aw." Jack unchained his bike and rode up the street, while the others pedaled as fast as they could to the bank.

When the group reached the bank, they saw a blue Mustang parked a block away from the bank. The men had changed the license plate. A man was leaning against the car.

"I'll distract him," Carly said. "You guys go in."

The boys hid in an alley and waited for Carly.

Carly dashed to the corner of the street, turned around, and screamed as loud as she could.

"Boy is she loud!" Sam remarked.

Hank heard the scream and looked over. Carly cried, "There's a bank robber here!"

"Hey!" Hank yelled, running after her.

Carly hopped on her bike, crossed the street, and rode away from the bank, Hank following.

"Do you think she'll be ok?" Jerry asked.

"She's a clever girl," Billy replied.

The boys left the alley and hurried to the bank.

"How do we get in?" Jerry asked, looking up at the building.

"The criminals must have gotten in through a window, cut the fuse box wires, then got to the

safe," Billy reasoned. "One of them might have had a job here sometime before the robbery to know where the fuse box was located."

"Does that answer my question?"

Billy shrugged.

Billy led the trio around the side of the building. A ladder was leaning against one of the second floor windows.

"That's where the men entered," Jerry pointed.

"So, who's going up first?" Billy asked.

When no one answered, Sam said, "Fine. I'll go."

As he climbed, Billy and Jerry held the bottom to keep it steady. After Sam swung into the window, Jerry climbed next.

When it was Billy's turn, he nervously tested each step before he put his full weight on them.

"Hurry up!" Jerry whispered hoarsely.

When Billy finally reached the top, Sam and Jerry helped him get inside.

"Now let's find the robbers." Sam turned on a flashlight.

The boys crept through the bank. Billy turned on his night vision goggles to help them dodge tripwires. The boys crawled up the stairs to the 4th floor, where they heard muffled noises from around a bend in the hall.

"The men are either using torches to burn their way through," Billy said, pushing his glasses up on his nose, "professional laser cutters, or they're expert safe crackers. By now they must have gotten inside the safe."

The boys heard footsteps echo through the hallway. They hid inside an office by the staircase. A tall man walked through the doorway with a white sack over his shoulder. Sam sprang from his hiding place and jumped the robber, trying to silently bring him to the ground.

The robber tried to grab his gun, but Billy and Jerry jumped on top of him. Sam pulled the gun from his holster while Jerry grabbed his pepper spray. He sprayed the man in the face, then put a hand over his mouth.

"What do we use to tie him up?" Sam asked, stuffing a cloth in the robber's mouth to gag him.

Jerry took off his sweater and gave it to him. They tied up the man's hands, then slid him into a room.

"Now it's time to set up some traps," Jerry said.

Billy took a bucket out of his backpack. "I'll retrieve some hot water."

Jerry took two cords out of his pocket, and handed one to Sam. Jerry tied his cord to a doorknob on one side of the hall. Sam took a small step-stool from Jerry's backpack and, standing on the stool, flung his cord over a light fixture and let it hang down the other side.

Billy soon came back with his bucket. Jerry stuck a finger into the bucket to test the water. A second later, he yelped and withdrew his hand. "Not boiling water! You'll seriously injure one of the robbers!"

"Oh, sorry." Billy grinned sheepishly. "I'll get some cooler water."

A minute later, Billy came back. Jerry tested the water again. This time, it was hot enough to be uncomfortable, but not painful. "Much better."

Sam tied one end of his cord to Billy's bucket, then hoisted it toward the ceiling. The boys then crouched inside a small office across the hall from where Jerry tied his cord.

After a few minutes, a masked person walked down the hallway in the boys' direction.

"What's taking Lark so long?" asked someone from around the corner.

"Yeah, he's supposed to be helping us carry the rest of the loot," said another.

"Get ready to fight them," Sam whispered to the boys. "Once they're on the floor, we'll drop the bucket and hose them down with pepper spray. Hopefully, we can stall them long enough until the police arrive."

"Are you sure this is a good idea?" Billy nervously pushed up his glasses.

"It's not," Sam answered, "but you and the others never listen to me, and I'm in charge of keeping you safe."

"We'll be fine," Jerry smiled. "It's a good thing we only have to tackle one big husky crook each."

"That's not very reassuring," Billy whispered.

"If this goes wrong, I'll hold them off and you two get out of here as fast as you can," Sam said.

When the robber started to pass the boys' hiding spot, Jerry pulled his cord tight.

Carly rode as fast as her bike could carry her away from the bank, Hank in hot pursuit. She tried to knock trash cans over into the smuggler's path, but it did little to stop him.

Soon, Carly came to a roadblock. Construction signs blocked the entire intersection. *Oh no!* Carly thought.

Carly looked over her shoulder and saw Hank's silhouette coming toward her. She jumped off her bike and ran into an alleyway

Carly hid in the shadows, waiting for Hank to arrive. But no one showed up. After a few minutes, Carly left the alley. There was no sign of the man. Hank had disappeared.

Carly started to walk back down the block, but Hank wasn't there. *I should get back to the bank,* she thought.

But as she crossed the street, rough hands wrapped around her shoulders. Carly struggled,

but was forced across the street. Carly looked up at her captor. It was Hank!

"Let me go!" Carly cried, kicking at Hank's legs.

Suddenly, several police sirens sounded. Hank shoved Carly away and tried to dash across the street, but two police cars blocked him. Four officers rushed out, handcuffed Hank, and put him into the car.

Jack exited one of the police cars and helped Carly to her feet. "Are you ok?"

"Yeah." Carly brushed herself off. "I volunteered to be the decoy."

"Now let's go stop those robbers," Jack said.

Jack and Carly got into one of the police cars, and they headed for the bank.

The robber tripped over Jerry's cord and onto the floor. Sam leaped from the office and pounced on the robber.

"Myles! DeWitt!" he cried.

The boys could tell by the voice that the robber was Wilson, the man with the briefcase.

Two men turned the corner, both carrying large white sacks. At the sight of the struggle, they ran down the hall to confront Sam. But as they passed the hiding spot of the boys, Jerry again pulled the cord. One of the robbers tripped and sprawled headlong to the floor. The other saw the trap, and turned to face the boys in the office. Billy then let go of the second cord. The bucket flipped over, dropping water on the third robber. He yelped and ripped off his black sweater.

"Quit crying, Myles!" Wilson shouted, obviously annoyed.

Jerry and Billy then rushed out of the office with cans of pepper spray in their hands, screaming loudly. They sprayed the surprised robbers with pepper spray. Dewitt was hit, but Myles dodged the spray, snatched the can away

from Jerry and threw it away, and tripped Jerry to the floor.

Sam had pinned Wilson's arms behind his back and was using his belt to tie the robber's wrists, but he saw Jerry go down. Sam let go of Wilson, slid across the floor, and kicked Myles in his shins, sending him sprawling to the floor.

But Wilson wasn't fully tied up. He ripped the belt off his wrists, stood, and lunged for Billy. Sam twisted, rolled, and flipped on the floor, trying to hold off all three robbers at the same time. "The plan is foiled. Run!"

Jerry and Billy turned and bolted for the stairs. Sam leaped to his feet, ducked under a swing from Wilson, and hurried after the boys.

"Get them!" DeWitt cried, still wiping pepper spray from his red eyes.

"Forget the kids!" Wilson objected. "Grab the money. We're outta here!"

The three boys raced down the stairs with Myles still chasing after them. But when they reached the first floor, they slammed straight into the police.

Pandemonium broke out as they all tumbled onto the floor. Myles managed to slip through the crowd of officers and bolted for the exit. But Jack, who was waiting outside with Carly and another police officer, stuck his foot out and tripped Myles. The officer handcuffed him and took him to a police car.

The Motorbike Gang told the officers all they knew about the robbery. Wilson and DeWitt had come with the money right then. At the sight of the police, they tried to run back upstairs, but they were quickly caught and handcuffed.

The police then brought down Lark, the man Billy, Jerry, and Sam had tied up.

"You're Frederick Clark," Jerry said as he was led past the gang. "The assistant branch manager

of the bank. That's how you got into the building and bank safe so easily."

Lark, or Clark, scowled at him.

The officers quickly escorted the robbers and boys to the chief, who was outside.

"Sir," an officer said to him, "we found these children in the bank. Apparently, they were fighting the bank robbers."

The chief looked at them with a puzzled expression on his face.

"Well, sir," Billy pushed up his glasses, "t-the department didn't believe our reports of smugglers a few days ago. We decided to, uh, take action ourselves, and, uh, delay their absconding until you arrived."

"What's absconding?" Carly asked.

"Not now," Jack muttered.

"We used mild chemical sprays and m-martial arts to, uh, prevent them from escaping

until you could, uh, apprehend them," Billy finished.

The chief looked baffled.

"Sir," an officer said, approaching the chief, "we have the robbers inside of the cars and we are ready to escort them to prison."

"Alright then," the chief replied. "But we also need to take our new heroes here for questioning as well." He smiled at the gang. "We'll call your parents and have them meet us at the station. They'll be in for a big surprise!"

# Chapter 13

At the police station, the gang told the authorities everything they knew about the case, including the names of the robbers. When their parents arrived at the station, they were baffled to learn they had captured bank robbers.

"So are you mad at us?" Carly nervously asked the adults once the interviews were over.

"Especially me?" Jack added, facing his mom.

The parents looked at each other.

"Well," Mr. Wesley finally answered, "We are concerned for your safety, and pretty upset that you all sneaked out of the hotel without us knowing, not to mention confronting bank robbers! And Jack, your mother told me about what you all have been doing. Sneaking to airports after school and following dangerous men without our knowledge is not approved." Mr. Wesley smiled. "But we're glad you're safe."

"Does that mean no punishment?" Jerry whispered to Billy as they left the station.

Billy smiled.

Mrs. Wesley looked at Jack. "We're going to have a long talk about detective work when we get home."

The next morning, the gang watched the news after breakfast. Every news channel the TV had was talking about the attempted bank

robbery and their courageous act. After a couple of minutes, Jerry turned off the TV.

"Everyone was talking about it during breakfast," Jack remarked.

"But the mystery isn't over," Billy said.

"What do you mean?" Sam asked from across the room. "We just stopped a *robbery*."

"We still have to disclose the location of the jewels. Since the men are criminals, we can safely assume their jewels are stolen goods as well."

They pondered the mystery for a moment.

"Didn't Wilson mention caves when he was at the bakery with Hank?" Carly asked.

"That's right," Jack answered. "And, he told someone during a phone call to move them to another cave after an incident."

"We *assume* he said to secrete them in a different cave," Billy corrected.

"What's secrete?" Carly asked.

"It means to hide or conceal."

"Ah."

"Wilson also told them to mark where they hid it," Jerry mentioned.

"But how will we know what cave they hid them in?" Jack asked.

"By the mark, obviously," Jerry said matter-of-factly.

"Like you know what the mark is," Sam retorted.

"Don't worry," Jack said, "I'm sure we'll figure this out."

"We won't," Sam said flatly.

The others ignored him and tried to think.

A few minutes later, Sam suggested, "The mark could be the diamond symbol!"

"Yes!" Billy agreed. "The mark was on Wilson's briefcase, his phony business card, his breakfast plate, and the threat message. It could be the gang's insignia, as well as symbols for messages. Great job, Sam."

"I thought you didn't want to solve the mystery," Jerry teased.

"It grew on me after a long while," Sam smirked.

"So, all we have to do now is find the caves," Carly said.

"But where would they be?" Jack asked.

"Maybe somewhere near the lake," Billy suggested.

"We'd better hurry," Carly reminded the others. "We only have one day to follow this lead."

"Then we need to go fishing," said Jerry.

The gang talked to their parents about the idea of going to the beach. The adults decided it was a good idea, so the boys changed and grabbed their things. The families drove down to the beach.

When they arrived, the kids enjoyed a light lunch before they started their quest.

"Let's hike up there." Jack pointed to a large sand dune toward the left end of the beach.

The kids jogged over and soon found dozens of hollows on one side of the dune. They ran over to investigate.

"We'll never find the jewels with all these caves," Jack moaned.

"We have to attempt to try," Billy said.

"Attempt to try?" Sam ruffled his little brother's hair.

The gang looked around, trying to find a mark in front of one of the cavities before they entered them.

Finally, Jerry called out, "I found something!"

The others rushed over to see what he had found.

"Look, a mark in the sand."

The mark looked like the diamond mark on Wilson's briefcase.

"Let's look inside." Jack stepped forward eagerly.

The others followed him into the cave, being careful not to disturb the roof. There were holes along the walls of the cave, big enough to fit things in them. They searched the holes, and soon, Billy found something.

"Hey guys, I've located a scrap of paper. Look at what it says."

The note read, "Evening Special," and had a green diamond mark next to it.

"What's 'Evening Special?'" Carly asked.

"It sounds like a restaurant deal," said Sam.

"Maybe you're right," Jerry replied.

"Let's search newspapers and ads for any shop that sells an evening special," Carly suggested.

"Good idea," the others agreed.

The gang raced back to the site where their parents had set up the picnic.

After building sandcastles, exploring other caves, and swimming, it was time to go. The families packed up and drove back to the hotel room. The gang then split up and began searching for evening specials.

Billy scanned the newspapers, going through one every 39 seconds. Jack and Carly searched the Web, and Sam and Jerry looked in shops across town.

After investigating for hours, the gang didn't find a restaurant with an evening special. Sam and Jerry came back to the hotel for dinner.

"Carly and I found nothing," Jack said glumly as they sat at a table.

"Same here," Jerry and Sam said.

"And I discovered nothing useful." Billy sighed, "even though I went through 72 newspapers, some dating all the way back to 1993."

"We'll have to continue tomorrow," Jack responded. "We've only got until tomorrow afternoon to find out where they are."

The gang ate in silence, trying to figure out a plan.

"We should ask the others to help," Carly suggested.

"They'll only find the same thing we did," Sam said. "Nothing."

After dinner, the kids headed back to their rooms. Before bed, Jack called the rest of the gang back home and updated them on the case.

"YOU DID WHAT?" Rachel replied when he told them about the bank robbery.

"That's awesome!" Mike cried.

"That's dangerous!" Rachel said at the exact same time.

"That's surprising," Robby said, at the same time as Mike and Rachel.

"I know, right?" Jack said, answering all of them. He then told them about the mystery of the diamond mark.

"Don't worry," Rachel said. "You'll find out the answer to the message before you leave."

"Try looking in Wilson's briefcase," Robby and Mike said at the same time.

"Right now it's time for bed," Jack answered, "but I'll try to look first thing in the morning. Goodnight."

The next morning, Jack and Carly walked down the hallway together as they hurried for breakfast. As they passed hotel rooms, they noticed the door to Wilson's room was open.

Jack snapped his fingers. "I almost forgot! Mike and Robby suggested that we look in Wilson's briefcase."

They quietly opened the door wider so they could enter the room, then closed the door behind

them. The room was empty except for a jacket on the desk chair and a suitcase underneath the bed. They grabbed the suitcase and put it on the bed. Inside were a few pairs of clothes and Wilson's briefcase. Carly pulled out the briefcase and put it on the desk.

"It's padlocked," Jack groaned.

"Wilson must not have wanted to take any chances after his papers spilled back home," Carly said, remembering the incident. "All we need to do now is find out the combination."

Jack thought. On a hunch, he put in the combination *B-G-R-Y*. The lock opened.

Carly stared open-mouthed. "How did you—"

"The diamond marks were four colors. In alphabetical order, they were blue, green, red, and yellow."

"Great job. You're starting to think like a real detective."

Jack opened the briefcase. Inside was a box-shaped radio. Jack took it and examined it. "This must have been the one he used to contact his friend," he said to Carly.

"But on which frequency?" Carly asked.

Also inside the briefcase was a map. Carly unfolded it and looked over it. One building had a green diamond mark drawn over it.

"That's the same mark that was at the cave," Jack noticed.

"And the building it's marking is this hotel!" Carly pointed.

The kids rifled through the stack of papers at the bottom of the briefcase, but, other than the papers Jack noticed back home, they couldn't make sense of the scrambled letters.

"They're probably written in code," Carly said.

They quickly put the items back into the briefcase and returned it to the suitcase. As they

were closing the suitcase, the door opened behind them. Jack and Carly spun around. One of the hotel staff members was standing in the doorway.

"What are you kids doing snooping in here?" he questioned angrily. "I don't care how many times you appear on the news, all rooms are off-limits except your own!"

Jack and Carly were speechless. Suddenly, the worker pushed them aside, grabbed the suitcase, and ran out of the room.

"Wait! He's the staff member Wilson was talking to!" Jack realized.

The kids raced after him.

The man rushed into the elevator and quickly closed it. Jack and Carly hurried down the stairs. The elevator hadn't opened yet.

"He might have gone into the basement," Carly guessed.

She ran to the basement while Jack stayed and watched the elevator. But as Carly opened the door, a security guard stopped her.

"Hey young lady, employees only." The man paused. "Hey, aren't you one of those kids on the news?"

"Yes."

Carly walked back over to Jack. "The basement is off-limits."

"And the staff member didn't come out on this floor," Jack replied glumly.

"Why don't we ask the receptionist for the 'Evening Special' now?"

Jack agreed. But as they started for the front desk, Carly suddenly stopped. "If the receptionist is working with the smugglers, he would know who we are from Wilson or one of the ring members."

"Which means he won't give us the jewels," Jack said disappointedly.

The kids thought for a moment.

"We can ask my dad to get them!" Jack bolted for the stairs. As Carly caught up, he added, "They'll never suspect an adult. Especially if he has the diamond mark."

Inside the Wesleys' room, Mr. Wesley was on his laptop.

"Dad, we need your help," Jack burst through the door.

"With what?"

"Getting stolen jewels!"

Dad got up from his chair. "Where are they?"

"The receptionist has them." Carly entered the room just then. "At least we think so. We need you to pretend you were sent by the smugglers to get them."

"Please, Dad?" Jack begged.

"I guess I can try."

Jack and Carly quickly explained the plan and helped Mr. Wesley disguise himself. The three

went to a nearby costume store and bought several items for Mr. Wesley to wear: a fake black beard, glasses, and a tan leather jacket. Once he was dressed, Mr. Wesley entered the front of the hotel and stopped at the front desk.

"Good morning, how can I help you?" the receptionist asked him.

"I'm interested in—" Mr. Wesley paused and looked around. He then finished in a low voice, "—the 'Evening Special.'"

"What do you know about that?" the man sneered.

Mr. Wesley slid the note with the diamond mark across the desk.

After looking at the slip of paper, the receptionist asked, "Did Wilson send you?"

Mr. Wesley hesitated, then nodded.

"One moment."

He reached into a drawer, and handed him a duffel bag.

"Now scram," he said in a low voice.

# Chapter 14

Mr. Wesley took the bag and went to the restroom. He quickly peeled off his beard, glasses, and leather jacket, then sneaked up the stairs to tell Jack and Carly about his success. Billy, Jerry, and Sam were also with them.

The group opened the duffel bag. Mr. Wesley took out blankets and clothes covering the contents. Underneath was a package with a label on it.

"The name on the package might be the company they were planning on selling them to," Billy suggested, pushing up his glasses. "Probably a foreign jewelry maker or museum."

Mr. Wesley opened the box. Enclosed were a dozen glittering jewels, each about the size of a golf ball. Half were blue diamonds, the others rubies and emeralds.

"We need to take this to the police right away," Jerry stated in awe.

"But a few of us need to stay here and make sure the receptionist and staff member don't slip out until the authorities arrive," Billy said.

"We still haven't found the pilot working with the ring, either," Carly mentioned.

"I'll take the jewels to the police," Jack said.

"No you won't," Mr. Wesley objected. "At least not by yourself."

"But that'll mean less guards on the employees."

"What if we call the police?" Sam suggested.

"It'd be safer if the jewels were in their hands," Jerry agreed.

"One of us could catch a taxi to the police station," Carly suggested.

"But who?" Billy asked.

"Mom could," Jack said. "I'll go get her."

Mrs. Wesley was with Mrs. Jones in the room next door. Jack opened the door. "Mom, we need to speak with you. It's urgent."

Mom looked at Mrs. Jones, then back at her son. "Ok."

When they got back to the Wesleys' hotel room, Jack blurted, "Mom, we need you to take some jewels to the police."

"What jewels?"

"Stolen jewels from California!"

He quickly explained the situation to her, and she agreed to the plan.

Jack and the others then hurried down the stairs. "I'll go with Mom, and the rest of you can block the receptionist and the staff member."

The group split up. But as Jack opened the lobby door, a hand grabbed him. Jack and Mrs. Wesley spun around, and saw the staff member with the receptionist.

"Give me those!"

The men grabbed the duffel bag, pushed them aside, and left the hotel. Jack's dad and his friends caught up to him and Mom, saw the men running away with the jewels, and chased after them.

The men ran to the taxi stop, where they attempted to hail a cab. But the group had caught up. The guys moved forward and jumped the smugglers.

Carly got the bag and tossed it to Mom and Jack. They caught it and jumped into the cab.

"To the police station, quick!" Jack shouted to the driver.

The taxi sped off, weaving through traffic. A few minutes later, it stopped at the station. Jack threw a ten-dollar bill at the driver, and he and Mrs. Wesley ran inside the building.

Meanwhile, Mr. Wesley and the rest of the gang were trying to hold off the smugglers at the taxi stop. During the fray, Carly was able to snap photos of the two men. The receptionist climbed out of the dogpile and ran down the street. Sam and Billy chased after him.

The staff member, the larger of the two, had broken free of Dad's grip. He headed back down in the direction of the hotel. Mr. Wesley, Jerry, and Carly chased after him. He turned left at the corner, and dashed through a few alleyways.

The trio were struggling to keep up with him. The man exited an alley and headed into the motel Hank had been staying at.

"I know where he's headed," Jerry said between breaths.

Carly radioed Jack. "Jack, we're at the motel by Lily's Bakery."

"Ok, Carly," Jack replied, "We're on our way with the police."

The three ran inside, where they saw the staff member getting on the elevator. Jerry ran for the stairs, Carly and Mr. Wesley right on his heels.

"He's headed for the third floor." Jerry said, taking the stairs three steps at a time.

When the trio got upstairs, the elevator opened. The staff member spotted them from across the hallway, and dashed for room 28. Mr. Wesley sprinted forward and brought him down with a swift tackle. They struggled for a moment,

but with Jerry's help, Mr. Wesley subdued the staff member.

Right then, the elevator opened. Several officers exploded down the hall and onto the staff member. Soon, they had him handcuffed. Jack and Mrs. Wesley hurried up the stairs.

"Where are Sam, Billy, and the receptionist?" Jack asked them.

"The receptionist ran off," Carly said, "so Billy and Sam followed him."

The police took the man downstairs.

"Why did the staff member come here if the robbers are in jail?" Jerry asked.

They thought for a moment.

"Which room was the man trying to get to?" Mrs. Wesley asked.

"Room 28," Jerry answered, "which was Hank's."

Mrs. Wesley started for room 28. The others followed.

"Why are you going in there, Mom?" Jack asked as she opened the door.

Mrs. Wesley started searching the room. "It's possible that they hid other stuff they stole here. That would explain why the staff member risked his capture to come here. He could have wanted to grab at least some of the money before he escaped."

She opened the closet door. Three white sacks and a small black bag stood on a high shelf. Mrs. Wesley grabbed one of the white sacks and opened it. There were several bundles of thousand dollar bills inside.

"Great job, Mom," Jack stared in amazement. "This proves that they were the ones who robbed the bank before we got here."

Carly grabbed the black bag, which contained several necklaces, rings, and gems. "This must be the stuff stolen from the jewelry shop."

Jerry grabbed the other sacks, and the group brought them to the sergeant.

"Good work," the sergeant said. "My men will try to find the other man and your friends."

"I hope it's not too late," Carly said.

# Chapter 15

Sam and Billy chased after the receptionist as he turned the corner. They followed him downtown, as he darted through the streets.

"We can't lose him," Sam said between breaths.

Billy was struggling to keep up with him. His legs felt like lead as they ran.

"Can we take a moment to recuperate?" he asked.

"What's recuperate?" Sam asked, mimicking Carly.

"Don't tease Carly," Billy scolded. "She's very inquisitive, which is a great character trait. Before long, she'll be talking like me."

Sam laughed. "Ok, sorry."

"So can we take a break?"

"Not until we stop the receptionist."

Sam and Billy ran through the busy streets, burning in the hot sun. But the boys couldn't keep up with him forever, and they eventually lost him in traffic.

"We'll never find him like this," Sam surveyed the intersection.

"Don't lose hope," Billy managed to say.

"Are you okay?"

"My leg muscles are exhausted, and so are my lungs."

After a brief rest, they spied the man walking into a building, and followed him. It turned out to

be Tony's Pizza Shack. As they entered, the man spotted them, and ran into the kitchen. Logan, the cashier, noticed the man's wary glance at the boys and dashed after him.

There was a loud crash in the kitchen as Sam and Billy entered. The receptionist was sprawled on the floor. Logan had thrown a large pizza pan to trip the man. Logan ran forward to capture him, but the receptionist shoved him into a stack of crates. The man made it to the back door and ran out, the cook yelling something in Italian. Sam and Billy hurried over to help him.

"Don't worry about me," Logan said. "Catch that dude!"

When the boys exited the restaurant, they saw the receptionist turn down into another alley. They ran after him, and turned into the small alley. They stopped at a brick wall.

"Dead end," Billy muttered.

The boys heard footsteps, and turned to see a figure shadowed against the darkness.

"Don't move," the receptionist ordered.

The boys raised their hands.

The receptionist moved toward them. He took the boys' watch and cellphone. "Let's go."

Billy and Sam complied. As they exited the alley, rain started to drizzle from the sky.

The three walked quickly, the receptionist trying to avoid any attention. Billy and Sam looked at each other in fright.

"You two squeal, and it's the last thing you'll do," he muttered.

The man led them to a car rental. Soon, he had rented a dusty PT Cruiser.

"Get in, quickly," he said to the boys.

They crawled into the back, and the car sped off.

The receptionist kept an eye on them through the mirror. Billy was seated behind the driver's

seat, so the receptionist had a limited view of him. Billy moved his hand to his left pocket and quietly removed his walkie-talkie. He lowered the volume to the lowest setting, and radioed Jack. He knocked on the cup holder next to him, tapping Morse code into the microphone of his walkie-talkie.

Billy knocked the words, "Billy, Sam, trapped, criminal, silver, PT Cruiser, Homer Avenue," then turned off the walkie-talkie. He hoped someone would understand.

Sam looked out the window. The receptionist had stopped at Lily's Bakery and now waited. After a few minutes of waiting, he picked up his phone and texted. Sam slowly leaned over to see what he was doing.

From reading the text, he learned that the man was waiting for someone, probably the staff member, but he hadn't shown up. Sam took a pen and an old receipt from his pocket, leaned over

subtly, and scribbled the phone number of the person the receptionist was texting. He showed it to Billy, who copied the number in case they would need an extra.

After a few more minutes of waiting, the receptionist pulled the car out of their parking spot and drove off.

But soon, the three could hear a loud siren.

"Argh," the man growled, slamming his fist on the dashboard. "The cops are here."

He accelerated the car, pressing hard on the pedal. The car lurched forward, putting distance between them and the police.

In response, the police cars split up, one turning left, one turning right, and one staying on the PT Cruiser's tail.

The receptionist kept his foot on the gas, twisting the steering wheel and swinging the car through the streets. He ran past stop signs and red

lights, several times almost crashing into other cars.

Suddenly, the other two police cars ambushed the receptionist, cutting him off on a highway that led outside of the city. The man swerved, scraping a nearby civilian car, and bumped the front right end of the Cruiser into a rail on the side of the road. Airbags blew up, hitting the man in his face.

The receptionist grabbed his gun and phone, ran out of the car, and hopped over the rail on the side of the highway into a forest. Four officers ran out of their cars and chased after the receptionist.

The Wesleys, Carly, Jerry, and two police officers ran over to the wrecked car. Fortunately, Billy and Sam were alright.

After getting the two boys out, the officers questioned them. Sam showed them the phone number he had copied.

"How did you guys find us?" Sam asked.

"Your brother told us where you were by sending Morse code to Jack's walkie-talkie," explained one of the officers.

Sam patted Billy on his shoulder.

"But the receptionist got away," Carly moaned.

"Let's set a trap for the receptionist and his friend," Billy said, a smirk sneaking up his face.

# Chapter 16

At the police station, Sam called the number as planned.

"Hello?" a voice on the other end answered.

Sam said in his deepest voice, "Listen. I have the jewels. If you want them, you'll have to pay."

"Who is this?"

"None of your business. If you want to see those jewels, you'll bring $80,000 to the park by Rosedale Hotel, in a picnic basket. I'm sure these jewels are worth more than that, and I have plenty of other people who want to buy them.”

“And where will the jewels be?” asked the stranger.

“I’ll bring them there in another basket. We’ll swap baskets, and I’ll even stay until you make sure they’re real.”

Sam hung up.

“Now we wait,” the police chief smiled.

“We need to get back to the hotel,” Jack said. “We’re taking a plane home at 1 o'clock this afternoon.”

“Well, it was nice working with you kids.” The chief shook hands with all five kids. “We’ll inform you when we catch the crooks.”

The gang said their goodbyes, then left the station. They took a taxi back to Rosedale Hotel. Upstairs, their parents were packing.

“Where were you all?” asked Jack’s mother. “You already captured the staff member.”

"Sorry we're late." Jack replied. "We were trying to capture the last two criminals involved with the robberies."

Mom looked at Dad, who shook his head and laughed.

"Well, come and help us finish packing. We're leaving in an hour."

After they finished, the families went downstairs to the food hall to enjoy their last meal at the hotel. The kids filled their plates with food and sat down at a table.

"I wish we weren't leaving yet," Jack sighed.

"The longer we stay, the more difficult it will be for us to cope with parting," Billy told him. "I, for one, had a pleasant time here. This was a good break from my laboratory."

"You mean Dad's garage," Sam corrected.

"It's my laboratory."

They all laughed.

After they finished, they went upstairs to collect their suitcases. Jack was the last to leave his room. He stood in the doorway, looking over the room one last time. His dad put a hand on his shoulder.

Jack grabbed the doorknob, and slowly closed it for the last time. The families grabbed their suitcases and walked downstairs to the front desk. After they checked out, they took the bus to the airport.

As they waited, Billy grabbed a magazine. Jack looked out the window of the building. He could see the city front, with its tall skyscrapers and short houses.

Soon, it was time to go.

As the group got up, Jack looked over the city one more time.

"Goodbye, Chicago," he said with a heavy heart.

They were soon sitting inside the airplane. Billy called Mike. After several seconds, a voice answered.

"Hi, Billy. What's up?"

"Greetings. We're on our way back to Westport."

"Hi, Mike," Carly said.

"How was your vacation?"

"It was awesome." Jack bounced on his seat, full of excitement.

"We caught the smugglers," Jerry told Mike.

"You did?"

"Yep, and the police are in an operation to catch two accomplices," Sam mentioned.

"That's great."

"We'll be back in Westport in a few hours," Jack said.

"Good. I'll tell Robby and Rachel the news. Treehouse out."

"I can't wait to get back to my lab," Billy wiggled in his seat. "I'll work on new technology for more mystery solving!"

"I doubt we'll have any more cases," Sam said.

"I think we will," Billy disagreed. He stood up and said, "Criminals, beware. The astounding Motorbike Gang is on the case!"

They all laughed.

"I'm glad school is over," said Jerry, "so we can relax once we get home."

"I, on the other hand, am not," Billy replied with a frown. "My education is worth every penny, much more than snoozing, anyway. 'Early to bed, early to rise, makes a man healthy, wealthy, and wise,' Benjamin Franklin said."

"Well Ben Franklin didn't understand the importance of a break."

They all laughed again.

Jack looked out the window of the plane. They were now flying above the clouds.

"Don't the clouds look like a giant blanket?" he asked the others.

"Either that or you're just tired," Carly replied with a chuckle.

Jack yawned, his eyelids fluttering before finally closing.

# Chapter 17

"Jack, it's time to get off the plane!"

Jack woke up. His mom was standing over him.

"Oh, sorry," Jack yawned.

Jack got up and stretched, then followed the others off the plane. After they got their luggage, they headed to the parking lot. They piled everything into their cars and drove home.

When the Wesleys got to their house, Jack brought his suitcase up to his room. He threw his suitcase onto his desk and jumped on his bed.

Jack laid there for a minute, letting his body readjust to his home. He went to the bathroom, showered, then went downstairs.

"Mom, I'll be at the treehouse!" he shouted on his way out the door.

"Just be home by 6 o'clock for dinner," she called back. "And you have mail!"

Jack opened an envelope from 'A Caring Citizen.' The letter read, "The E-Bikers are going to get revenge!"

Jack frowned, puzzled. He took his bike out of the garage and drove to Mike's house. He parked it in the driveway, chained it up, and knocked on the front door. Mrs. Michaels answered.

"Well, hello, Jack," she said with a smile. "Mike told me you and the others were back from your vacation. How was it?"

"It was great," Jack replied.

"Mike and a few others are in the treehouse."

"Thank you."

Jack ran out the back door to the treehouse. As he climbed up the ladder, Rachel greeted him.

"Hi, Jack."

"Hi, Rachel! It's good to see you."

Inside the treehouse, Billy, Sam, Mike, and Robby were sitting.

"I can't believe you guys actually solved a case," Mike said excitedly. "And I was right about the ring of smugglers!"

"Well, that's not entirely accurate," Billy corrected him.

"It was pretty close."

Shortly after the comment, Jerry and Carly arrived.

"Why is all the furniture damp?" Jerry noticed.

"Oh, that," Robby grinned sheepishly. "We had a giant fight with the E-Bike Gang. But—"

"But we won," interrupted Mike.

"Thanks to Billy's Gardenator 3000," Rachel added.

"See," Billy said to Jack, "my inventions aren't useless after all."

Jack groaned. "Ok, Billy. But don't start making rules about carrying tracking devices."

"I think we should continue to solve crimes," Carly said, changing the subject.

"I'm not sure," Rachel replied. "It's a very dangerous business. Besides, we could barely solve this one."

"Also," Billy stated, "it is unlikely we'll cross paths with any conspiracies again."

"In the meantime, why don't we clean up the treehouse?" Robby suggested.

Everyone groaned.

"Speaking of treehouses," Jack remembered, "this note was in my mailbox."

He pulled the note out from his pocket and showed it to the gang.

"Don't worry about the note," Mike said. "The E-Bikers are sulking from their defeat."

"Now, let's start cleaning," Robby said.

After an hour of cleaning, playing games, and hanging out, Jack looked at his watch.

"It's time for me to go home for dinner," he said to the others.

"Us, too," said Billy.

"Well, if everyone's finished, the meeting will be adjourned."

The gang all said goodbye, then split up on their bikes and headed home. Jack parked his bike in the garage, then went inside his house, washed his hands, and sat down for dinner.

"So, how did you like the vacation?" asked Mom.

"It was great," Jack said. "We actually solved a crime. And the police chief will call us when they catch the last two crooks."

"I can't believe you and the others actually caught the smugglers." Dad said, still a little surprised at the feat.

"You and Mom helped, too."

"But we're not happy that you snuck out of the hotel to do it," Mom said.

Jack put his head down. "Sorry about that."

"We won't bring it up again," Mom said.

Just then, the phone rang. Jack sprang out of his seat to get it before Mom or Dad could stop him. Jack answered the phone.

"Hello?"

"Is this Jack?"

"Yes."

"This is Chief Crawford of the Illinois State Police. We have successfully captured the last two accomplices. Well done, Jack."

Jack leaped in the air in excitement.

The chief said that the ring made a full confession. Wilson admitted to stealing the jewels from California with Frederick Clark, who was away from Chicago "on vacation," and DeWitt. They loaded the jewels onto a small motorboat and sneaked away into the Pacific Ocean. The pilot picked them up with his seaplane and planned to bring them to Chicago, but stormy weather and low fuel made them land in Michigan.

Hank, Myles, the receptionist, and the hotel staff member had robbed the bank the night before Wilson got to Chicago. Hank admitted to committing the jewelry theft the day after the bank robbery. He wasn't satisfied with his cut of

the money and didn't know Wilson was planning another robbery.

When Wilson ran into Jack again in Chicago, he really became concerned and sent some of the ring to kidnap him and his friends. But in the big city, there were almost always people around, so a kidnapping was nearly impossible.

The ring decided to forget the gang and rob another bank. But they realized their mistake too late and were captured by the police. The receptionist, the staff member, and the pilot planned on a jailbreak once the jewels and money were secured, but their plans were disrupted when Mr. Wesley got the jewels. The staff member was captured, and the other men were lured into a trap.

Jack thanked the chief, then hung up. After telling his parents the news, he called each member of the gang to tell them about the call from the chief.

After dinner, Jack took a shower and headed to bed.

A week later, as Jack was watching TV, Mom came into the living room with the mail. "Jack, there's a letter for the Motorbike Gang."

Jack took the envelope, surprised, as the gang had never gotten mail before.

Jack called his friends on his smartwatch, summoned a meeting, and drove to the treehouse. After everyone arrived, he showed them the letter. It read,

*Dear Motorbike Gang,*

*The city of Chicago and state of California would like to thank you for your involvement in the capture of the ring of smugglers. We appreciate your bravery and courage and would like to congratulate you on your investigation.*

Jack pulled out a check from the envelope. "A hundred dollars?!"

The entire gang cheered.

Carly took the check and danced around, whooping in delight. "This is amazing!"

"I want my share," Sam said. "You know how much work I did watching you guys?"

"But we have to split the money with Mike, Robby, and Rachel," Jerry said. "Without Rachel's help, we wouldn't have gotten the supplies needed to capture the robbers. And without Robby and Mike, we probably wouldn't have

searched Wilson's briefcase and found the jewels."

"Ok," Jack said, "we'll share."

"Great," Billy said. "Now, if you'll excuse me, I need to start working on some more spy gear. I want to be prepared for another mystery."

# Acknowledgements

The Chicago Bank Robberies would not have been possible without the Lord giving us the idea and sending us the people who took the time to edit, review, encourage and give feedback for our manuscript:

We extend a very special thank you to Mrs. Ellen Byham for her generous contributions as a developmental editor.

We humbly appreciate Mrs. Darlene Catlett for taking her time to thoroughly copyedit.

We cherish the wisdom and mentorship we received from Coach Terry Travers.

We are encouraged by Ms. Janyce Brawn's kind words and recommendations after reviewing our manuscript.

We are grateful for the feedback and suggestions given by our beta readers:

Alex Kocsis, Isaac Bolander, Jabin and Elese James, and Mrs. Jen Roberson. Especially the suggestion given by Elese James to add more girls to the story.

And thank you to everyone else who supported us in any other kind of way.

# About The Authors

Matthew Pierre is a young author who enjoys reading, writing, playing sports, practicing piano, and graphic design.

Zachary Pierre is an aspiring computer scientist who likes to spend his time writing, reading, drawing/painting, or playing with his dog.

The idea for *The Motorbike Gang* originally came from brothers Matthew and Joshua but was eventually written by Matthew and Zachary. The series teaches traditional family values and promotes healthy relationships and Christian behavior.

To learn more, visit mattandzachwrite.com